W9-ACR-889

HOME TO ROOST

HOME
TO
ROOST

Andrew Garve

Thomas Y. Crowell Company
NEW YORK ESTABLISHED 1834

ASBURY PARK PUBLIC LIBRARY
ASBURY PARK, NEW JERSEY

Copyright © 1976 by Andrew Garve

All rights reserved. Except for use in a review, the reproduction or utilization of this work in any form or by any electronic, mechanical, or other means, now known or hereafter invented, including xerography, photocopying, and recording, and in any information storage and retrieval system is forbidden without the written permission of the publisher.

Designed by Ingrid Beckman

Manufactured in the United States of America

Library of Congress Cataloging in Publication Data

———

Home to roost.

I. Title.
PZ3.W7354Hp3 [PR6073.I56] 813'.9'12   76-3521
ISBN 0-690-01141-5

10 9 8 7 6 5 4 3 2 1

BOOKS BY ANDREW GARVE

HOME TO ROOST

I

This is an account of how Max Ryland got himself murdered, and what happened afterward. For obvious reasons, the manuscript will not see the light of day until all
the people concerned are dead and forgotten; I have
taken steps to ensure that. You may think, dear future
reader, that as a story it builds up rather slowly—but so
does a hurricane. I am setting it down because I played a
big part in the drama—just *how* big will become apparent
to any perceptive person prepared to soldier on to the
end.

My name is Walter Haines. It's a rather ordinary sort
of name, I'm afraid, but that is what I was landed with.
At the start of this writing I am thirty-five years old, five
feet nine inches tall, and about ten stone in weight,
which means I'm on the skinny side. I have a thatch of
slightly nondescript brown hair, all my own teeth, and
no special distinguishing marks. I am not what anyone

would call a fine specimen of manhood, and I'm certainly not handsome, though my features are agreeable enough not to frighten small children. (Self-depreciation—that old fault! I must try to avoid it.)

I was born in Leicester of middle-class parents (there I go again!), and through them I inherited a more than usually mixed bag of traits.

Take one of them. My maternal grandfather was a machinist; my paternal grandfather was a builder and decorator in a small way of business. Their manual skills and practical interests skipped a generation with my parents, but they were to come out strongly in me, as my story will show.

My father was an idealist who spent his life working for causes, many of them unpopular at the time. The causes he espoused were mainly three—the temperance movement, socialism, and the Methodist church, of which he became a pillar. He was also an ardent pacifist, an antivaccinationist, and a believer in nature cures and health foods. In short, he was a bit of a crank. However, he was by no means a negligible crank, and in the end he became something of a national figure. He was a gifted organizer, a master of detail in his subjects, a speaker and debater of the first order—and he proselytized with tireless energy. He had no doubt whatever that he was on the side of right against wrong, a conviction which his opponents found irritating. As a youth I was much under his influence, both by genes and upbringing, and I walked proudly in his large shadow. His moral courage was never in doubt; his physical courage, as far as I know, was never tested. I now have the feeling that while he would have faced bravely—and even have welcomed—the minor martyrdom of jail for his faiths, he would have flinched from anything more painful.

We were, of course, always poor. The organizations he served had little money, and the free-lance journalism by which he supplemented his income was an erratic provider. He seemed not to mind, or even notice, our poverty, for his own material wants were eccentrically few. He was, without doubt, a very contented man, as he worked away in his tiny cluttered room in our home, absorbed, preoccupied, and detached.

My mother, who shared—or seemed to share—my father's basic views, was wholly different from him in temperament. She was impulsive, emotional, and creative. She enjoyed writing poetry; she read papers at literary societies; and she made up entrancing fairy stories to tell me nightly by the fireside when I was small. She gave color and warmth and feeling to my early life. She was a good-looking woman, though her face in repose was sometimes strangely sad. Perhaps it was just her cast of feature; or perhaps, as I have lately come to believe, my father concentrated too much on his causes and not enough on her. One knows little of the intimate life of one's parents.

I started my working life as a newspaper reporter. I had had an itch to write since quite early days, and I took a job on the *Leicester Gazette* under the impression that reporting and writing were in some way connected. This, of course, was an error. I sooned learned that a man can be a good reporter without even being literate—and vice versa. I also discovered that temperamentally I wasn't suited to the job. To be a good general reporter, you need to be tough and thrusting, and I was neither. I stuck it out for several years, but the rough-and-tumble did get me down a bit at times. I was hopeless at covering fires, where conditions were usually chaotic and facts were hard to come by. I never mastered the art of extracting information from policemen on duty. There was a reporter in the office, a shambling man of fifty who looked rather like a worn-out cop himself, who would sidle up to a policeman, say something out of the corner of his mouth, and in a few moments have the "lowdown" on the story. I did my best to imitate him, but got nowhere. I was always told to "Move on!" Once, even more humiliatingly, it was "Move on, sonny!" I suppose I just didn't have the presence.

There were many other jobs that I hated, though of course I had to do them. I didn't enjoy calling at a mortuary and having a bullet-riddled body drawn out on a tray for my inspection. I didn't enjoy interviewing bereaved relatives after a murder or a suicide. I was terrified when a line of mounted police charged past me at full gallop into a rioting mob. I suffered nightmares after being sent to cover a gruesome train wreck.

However, looking back, I don't regret any part of those reporting days. They forced me to overcome, if only temporarily, the diffidence of a naturally retiring disposition. They schooled me to look at flowing blood and not fall flat on my face in a faint. They taught me where and how to gather information, an invaluable asset to me later on. They encouraged resourcefulness and self-reliance, qualities I was short of. They gave me an immense amount of useful knowledge and experience—particularly of the world of crime, which interested me. What I really wanted to do was to write books—preferably crime books. I had managed to produce a couple of full-length stories in my spare time, while I was at the *Gazette*, and both had been published, with modest success. So I knew that I *could* write—and in my late twenties I decided to take a chance, throw up the job, and apply myself full time to the writing of detective and adventure fiction, in what I hoped would be the stimulating atmosphere of London.

It was a hard slog to start with. I lived and worked in a squalid bed-sitter in Camden Town, and it was a problem sometimes to keep body and soul in proximity. I typed like a maniac from morning till night, and as far into the night as my landlady would allow. In order to survive, even at the most meager level, I had to turn out four or five books a year under different names. They were of fair quality as action stories, but they were certainly not great literature. My strength, so far as I had any, lay in constructing tortuous and ingenious plots, with unusual backgrounds and a meticulous attention to detail. A loose end to me was like a botched-up bit of joinery to a cabinetmaker. My weakness was in portraying people. At that time I rarely gave any thought to the workings of my *own* mind, let alone to the minds of others. I was much more interested in the mechanics of a plot, the fitting together of the pieces, than in the mental processes of the people involved in it. As a result, my characters tended to be from stock and rarely came to life as individuals. They were there merely to fill the roles that the story required. It was a grave defect in a writer. I would probably have failed as a professional and been forced to go back to some regular job if it hadn't been that, just over five years ago, I had an enormous stroke of luck. A story entitled *Death at the Summit*, an international spy thriller with a lot of action, a nice twist in the middle, and a denouement in the High Alps, happened to catch the public fancy. Its fast-moving narrative and technical expertise evidently more than made up, in the readers' view, for any lack of depth in the characters—and the book took off. It was serialized in Britain and America; it was bought for translation into more than a dozen languages; and it was filmed by a top company with a galaxy of stars in the leading parts. Hardcover and paperback sales were fantastic, and in a few months I had become—even allowing for taxes—a comparatively well-to-do man. I had also become something of a celebrity. I was interviewed, and photographed, and written about in magazines, and several times I was invited to appear on the telly or the radio to air my views on literature, art, politics, morality, and the state of the world. I didn't take happily to the limelight, but it seemed sensible to cash in while the going was good.

It was during this brief period of fame, when the aura of success was around me, that I had an even greater stroke of luck. I met Laura Franklin. I was about to be interviewed on BBC TV, and Laura was the makeup girl who touched up my face for the cameras. She was an attractive brunette with an absolutely stunning figure, and as she delicately penciled my rather scanty eyebrows, I saw with surprise that she wore no ring. We didn't have long together, but conversationally we covered quite a bit of ground. She knew who I was, of course, and she'd read *Summit* and found it exciting, and though she must have met lots of far more famous people in her line of work, she showed an interest in me which I felt went well beyond the call of duty. It suddenly struck me that this could be one of those tides in the affairs of men . . . I took a deep breath and asked her if she'd care to lunch with me sometime. Without hesitation she said she'd be delighted to, and there and then we made a date.

What followed differed little from the common experience, though at the time, naturally, I felt it was something unique in the annals of the human race. We met, and met again, and yet again, at rapidly diminishing intervals, fanning the initial spark into a glow. We talked about ourselves and each other, about our work and our interests. Laura asked the questions that most people ask of authors—though, coming from her, they seemed almost original—and for once I was eager to answer them. She wanted to know whether I worked regular hours or waited for inspiration, whether I typed all my stuff myself and with how many fingers—I held up one on each hand—and where I got my ideas from. She was genuinely curious, so I gave her a short rundown on a professional writer's life. I said that a successful author was in many ways a very fortunate man. He had no boss to give him instructions. He could write what he liked. He was out of the rat race, the daily commuting, the crowds and the crush. He was as independent as anyone could be on this earth. But of course that didn't mean that he could live without discipline—his self-discipline had to be brutal. He had to force himself to go to his desk and do his stint whether he felt like it or not. "Anyone who writes only when the mood takes him," I said, "is heading straight for the poorhouse." And I said that more or less the same thing applied to ideas. It was no good hoping for a sudden flash of inspiration—there were few "Eurekas" in the writing business. Maugham's advice was the best— "Apply the seat of the pants to the seat of the chair." And stay on it—reflecting on possibilities, letting the fancy range, allowing one thought to suggest another—until in the end something emerged.

Laura listened with flattering attention while I talked. Afterward, I got her to tell me about her own job. She was very modest about it—"I'm only one of the girls, you know, not a supervisor or anything grand like that"—but she was obviously proud of her niche. She said the job wasn't nearly as glamorous as some people thought—particularly on location on an icy morning when your fingers were all thumbs and the makeup was too cold to go on smoothly. Actually you had to be very tough and fit, because there was usually a time schedule to be met and the pace could be hectic, and if you didn't love the work, you'd never stick it. But there was also excitement and involvement and sometimes the feeling that you'd played a tiny part in creating an artistic triumph, which was very satisfying.

We exchanged, quite early on, *curricula vitae*. I told Laura of a scholarship that had taken me to a Leicester grammar school, of another scholarship that had given me three years at university, of an Eng. Lit. degree that had been the subject of some ribald mirth at the *Gazette*, of my reporting days and my early struggles as a writer. I told her about my parents, still alive and still living in Leicester, and quite a bit about my eccentric father, now withdrawn from active public life but currently busy ghosting the autobiography of a certain Miss Strang, a noted temperance reformer, to be entitled "People I Have Met and Places I Have Seen"! I learned in turn that Laura was twenty-four, six years younger than I;

that she had attended the Ecole des Beaux Arts in Paris; that she had worked briefly as a "beautician"—dreadful word!; that her father, who had been an architect, had recently died; that her mother had settled in Bath and opened a boutique there; that Laura was an only child, as I was.

At each successive meeting she seemed to me more attractive, more desirable. She had laughing sepia eyes, an infectious vitality, a quick intelligence, a mental and physical liveliness that I found enormously engaging. . . . But why strain for words to describe the indescribable? In simple terms, I had fallen head over heels in love with her. And, however improbable it may seem in retrospect, she had fallen for me.

Once the mutual declarations were made—which was soon—we moved quickly. We were both free to marry; we both wanted to; and there were no financial or other impediments. I met Laura's mother, and Laura met my parents, in the old-fashioned way, and exactly six weeks after the eyebrow-penciling session, we were married without fuss at a Kensington registry office, neither of us being a churchgoer. Laura was accompanied by a close friend, Muriel Entwisle, about whom more later, and I rustled up a bloke I'd known from university days to balance the party. We had a family celebration afterward, and then Laura and I flew off to Tobago for what turned out to be an idyllic three-week honeymoon.

Soon after we got back to London, we bought a house. The comfortable Belgravia flat I'd been living in since my financial bonanza was hardly big enough for the two of us, and in any case Laura thought she would enjoy having a small garden. The house we chose was a rather splendid affair, built into a hillside on the outer edge of London's northwestern suburbs. It was called Green Boughs, a pleasant-sounding name which we saw no reason to change. The property was spacious without being huge; it was well separated from its nearest neighbors—"secluded but not isolated" was the agent's phrase—and it had a large double garage for our two cars, with a section at the back for tools and outdoor furniture, and a large rear door leading conveniently into the garden. Best of all, it had an uninterrupted view over treetops and protected greenbelt to the open country. I had always had a hankering to live somewhere high up, to be able to look down instead of along, and this view was really superb. The attractive and very private garden, walled on both sides with rosy brick, was mostly lawn with small herbaceous borders, and Laura thought it looked manageable as well as inviting. In short, we were both delighted with our purchase. An additional advantage of the place was that though it gave the impression of being deep in rural England, it was actually only ten miles from Central London, with a handy choice of underground stations. By car on a day of average traffic, it was barely thirty minutes from Piccadilly.

We made a few small changes at the house before we moved in, the most important being to the room I was to use as a study. I happen to have an abnormally acute sense of hearing, and the slightest external sound can break the thread of my thought when I'm working. I had tried ear plugs, but they hadn't proved very satisfactory. When I was plugged up, I could hear my own heart beating, which was reassuring but not comfortable. My Belgravia flat had had double windows, which had kept some of the noise out. Now I arranged for similar windows to be installed in the new study. They wouldn't afford much protection against a road drill or a generator, but they would deaden any ordinary sounds.

Laura had continued with her BBC job in the first months after our marriage, but as soon as we moved to the house, she gave it up. She pointed out, with obvious sense, that being the wife of a writer working at home was quite different from being the wife of a man who left for his office at nine in the morning and didn't get home till seven. There would be no problem for her of long, lonely days to fill, since I would be around all the time; and I certainly couldn't be expected to look after myself. In our rare and privileged circumstances, she would positively enjoy being a housewife. As I would enjoy her being it, too, there was really nothing more to be said.

It didn't take us long to establish a satisfactory domestic and working routine. I would shut myself away in the study soon after nine o'clock, and write till one. Laura would do the chores as quietly as possible, tiptoeing around in order not to disturb me. I felt rather bad about her having no help in the house, particularly in view of its size, but she agreed with me that a daily woman might be noisy and distracting, and insisted she was quite able to cope, as indeed she was. At lunchtime we would often eat at a local restaurant, which cut down the shopping, and which we both enjoyed; and then spend the afternoon together, perhaps strolling in the greenbelt or going to a cinema or just occupying ourselves companionably in the garden or the house. I would work again between six and eight, and Laura would cook the evening meal. She wasn't a terribly good cook, and she knew it, but as I told her with a tolerant smile, she would probably improve with practice. I had done a bit of cooking myself in my bachelor days, and I showed her how to prepare some of the dishes.

Considering how superficially we had known each other at the time of our marriage, and with what headlong speed we had taken the plunge, it was largely luck that—apart from being deeply in love—we found so much in common. The writing scene was still new to Laura, and she was intrigued by every aspect of it. She shared with me the pleasures and pains of the morning post—the new contracts, the exciting film offers that so often came to nothing, the unexpected checks, the snide reviews, the fan mail. Some of the letters annoyed us; some made us laugh; some reduced us to giggles. As when my agent, commenting on my one pathetic attempt to write a mystery play, wrote, "It is slightly ironical that the only time there is any action in the play is when it takes place in the dark where nobody can see it." As when my publisher wrote, "I am not sure that you want your hero in bed with a nymphomaniac by page three." As when a railway enthusiast complained bitterly that a train I had mentioned as starting from Fenchurch Street station would in fact have started from St. Pancras. As when, after I had written a story with an exciting canoeing sequence, I was invited by a man in Arizona to shoot the rapids of the Colorado River with him. Yes, we enjoyed our mail. Laura read all the reviews carefully— much more carefully than I, since criticism tended to depress me—and she would sometimes come sparkling to me with a gem of contradiction. One of her choicest items was a clash of opinion, between two American reviewers, about the same book on the same day. One of them wrote, "A weak British entry, starting off nicely but bogging down in artificial suspense, and lacking both credibility and inventiveness." The other one wrote, "After an unpromising start, this one gathers speed to a smashing climax and convincing finish." We had a good chuckle over that.

Laura enjoyed discussing ideas and plots with me, and reading the various drafts when I was ready to show them to her, and even offering tentative suggestions now and again. Of course, any creative work is basically an individual thing, and I did jokingly recall on one occasion the old crack, "A camel is a horse created by committee." However, she was sometimes quite helpful. She was certainly good at thinking up small human touches to give my literary puppets more life. She also had a good ear for dialogue, for people talking out of character, for the various ways in which different kinds of people framed their sentences—and though I may not always have sounded grateful (authors rarely welcome even the most constructive advice), I took private note of her suggestions and quite often slipped in a minor change.

Work was by no means the only point where our interests coincided. Our small domestic hobbies went well together. One of my relaxations, for instance, was carpentry. I had discovered an aptitude during my school days, but had had little opportunity to indulge the taste since. Now I could saw and chisel and plane to my heart's content, and I found it very therapeutic. Though still creative, it occupied the hands while resting the mind. Just getting my overalls on and my bag of tools out refreshed and cheered me. During our first spring I had a load of timber delivered from a nearby yard and built a small summerhouse at the bottom of the garden— naturally with Laura's approval—where we would be able to sit and sunbathe even in quite cool weather. It was a fairly rough job by professional standards, but Laura admired it and said she would like to put the creosote on. So I opened the tin for her and showed her which brush to use, and she contributed her mite. During the building of the summerhouse she had busied herself in the garden; keeping the lawn trimmed, and weeding, and burning rubbish in the incinerator when the wind was right, so that we were pleasantly occupied together, chatting away as well as improving the homestead. Laura also did some sketching and painting in the garden that spring, setting up her easel close to where I was working. She produced, I thought, some rather odd results, but at least it meant that we were able to spend a lot of time together in nonwriting hours, companionably engaged in our pursuits.

Perhaps the best times we had were when a book was finished, and the next one not yet thought of, and we were as free as any human beings in the world could be. In those quite long periods, sometimes lasting for many weeks, we were constantly off somewhere, constantly on the move. I had got rid of my car, an MG, since we had Laura's Rover for town use, and had bought instead a secondhand station wagon, American and very large, which was good for rough country tracks and for carrying gear, and which could even be slept in at a pinch. We used it regularly for picnics in the Chilterns and day runs to the coast, and frequently for longer trips to some place that sounded attractive, some district that we hadn't yet explored. I remember we had a splendid couple of weeks in the Lakes one gorgeous May, before the swarming crowds had taken over. I'm no rock climber—the expertise in *Death at the Summit* was all researched—but I en-

joyed our adventurous scrambles on the fells, and so did
Laura. Perhaps too much—she seemed to have no fear. I
was quite concerned for her on Hellvellyn's precipitous
Striding Edge, vividly imagining a false step and its
awful consequences, and I went protectively ahead,
pointing out the more difficult bits before she came to
them and warning of loose stones. In fact she got through
without trouble—laughingly, in the end, because it was I
who stumbled as I turned to indicate a damp patch and
give her a helping hand. In those two weeks we climbed
five peaks of nearly three thousand feet, and I still have
the staff on which I cut the names and dates as a record
of achievement.

At least once a year, and usually in the worst of the
winter months, we traveled abroad. These were memorable trips. We went to Greece and Crete and Rhodes; we
cruised to Turkey and visited Troy and Ephesus; we
took the station wagon to Spain and the Camargue and
Provence; we sailed through the Panama Canal to San
Francisco in one of the last of the great P. & O. liners,
and crossed the southern United States by Greyhound
bus in a January heat wave; and several times we went on
business trips to New York. I was never quite as carefree
on these journeys as Laura, since all the places were po-
tential backgrounds for stories, with scenes to be memo-
rized and notes to be jotted down. However, there was
no feeling of immediate pressure, so most of the time I
was a reasonably good companion.

I may have given the impression that Laura and I
spent those early years entirely in each other's pockets—
but this was by no means the case. During my periods of
active writing, when I could think of nothing but getting
on with the story, Laura was able to cultivate her sepa-

rate interests and meet her many friends. Everyone liked Laura—everyone felt better for seeing her. She was a shot in the arm, a surge of adrenaline, a blood transfusion. Wherever she went, she was welcomed. And she went quite a bit. She was a very sociable person, a mixer, an outgoing type—the exact opposite of what I had thankfully reverted to after leaving the *Gazette*. She would make sure that I was well supplied with food and all requirements, and then drive into town to lunch and shop and gossip with her girl pals—perhaps dropping in to a matinee or a gallery or some exhibition she had read about. She had enormous gusto for such things. She realized she was fortunate to have these opportunities while I was slogging away at home, but I didn't grudge her her pleasures—indeed, I told her I was glad she was being kept happy. The one thing that did worry me a little about her excursions was that she *would* always take the car instead of going in by underground. It was true that she had been driving for years with only an occasional minor incident, but she always seemed to me to lack road sense, and I was never wholly easy in my mind until she returned. When we were in the car together, I always took the wheel, as a matter of course. I knew that if she drove, I'd be tense, with hands gripping the seat arms and feet pressed hard down on the floor. When I drove, I was relaxed, and so was she. So obviously it was the sensible arrangement.

We did quite a bit of entertaining at home, particularly in the early years of our marriage. Laura loved having people, although she was very good about not inviting anyone when the writing heat was on. Most of the guests were friends of hers from the BBC days, or people she had come to know in the neighborhood and had introduced to me. Laura picked up friends like a magnet picks up iron filings. I didn't mind seeing these people once the first meeting was over and the ice was broken; it was the new encounters that I rather dreaded. Naturally I preferred having people come to us rather than the other way around—which involved much more effort, at least for me. Of course we couldn't altogether avoid return visits, but Laura had learned to make plausible excuses on my behalf, so we managed to keep them to a minimum.

Our most frequent visitor, and the person I saw most of apart from Laura, was Muriel Entwisle, whom I've mentioned as attending the wedding. She and Laura had met on a holiday cruise a year or two before our marriage, and a close and very stable friendship had developed. Muriel was older than Laura—she was nearer my own age. She was a doctor, a GP not a specialist, sharing a group practice in Paddington with another woman and two men. They had joint premises for their surgery, but Muriel's plate was also up at a neighboring flat where she lived alone. She was a big woman, large-boned, heavy around the shoulders, and decidedly plump. I suspected that she secretly consumed the carbohydrates she forbade to others. She was a jolly person, very good company, highly intelligent and knowledgeable, full of sound common sense, and rather motherly toward Laura.

I liked Muriel, and had no reason to suppose that she didn't like me. She certainly gave the impression that she admired my work. All the same, there were times when I felt less than comfortable with her. As the three of us sat and chatted after a meal, I would catch her eyeing me in a disconcertingly appraising way. It was as though she didn't wholly approve of me, as though she were reserving judgment about me. She was by nature outspoken—far more so than Laura when it came to personal matters—but she was careful never to criticize me. Of course, when we came to know each other really well, she would sometimes tease me about my little foibles.

I remember, for instance, one Sunday morning in April when she dropped in for a prelunch drink, very cheerful, and quite ecstatic about the beautiful spring day. "Yes," I said, "but I'm afraid it's not going to last"—which was true, because I'd just tapped the barometer and it had gone down with a bang. She laughed, and so did Laura. "That's our Walter!" Muriel said. "Always meeting troubles halfway." And Laura said, "He can't help it, Muriel; he's just a born pessimist. A belt-and-braces man. *His* bottle is always half empty, never half full. I've got used to it."

"I open my eyes in the morning," I said. "You can't get more optimistic than that." But it was merely a joke I'd heard. I knew that I did have a tendency to look on the dark side, to anticipate trouble, to expect the worst. I couldn't pick up a book in a shop without wondering if the store detective's eye was upon me. I was always ready for the train to crash, the bridge to collapse, the tree to come down across the road in front of me. It was, I supposed, something to do with having imagination, with being a writer. *My* sort of writer, anyway. After all, crime and disaster are pretty closely linked.

"At least," I said, "if you expect the worst you're not disappointed when it happens. Personally, I regard pessimism as a sensible insurance. . . . Now how about getting that half-empty bottle even emptier?" It was all very good-humored.

On another occasion, though, I thought I detected a

slight cutting edge to Muriel's badinage. I had been troubled in my study by the distant hum of our central-heating boiler, and had told Laura that we really must try to have something done about it. Laura mentioned this difficulty to Muriel. Muriel gave me one of her odd looks and said, "Have you ever thought of trying to ignore it?". I said, "Yes—but it doesn't work." "It might if you persisted," she said. "Pretend it's not there. Decide to take no notice of it. Or better still, tell yourself you like it—that it's a homely background sound which you'd miss. Then you'll probably stop hearing it."

It was the nearest Muriel had ever come to lecturing me. I made a face at her, and changed the subject.

II

I would say, looking back, that Laura and I had three very happy years together before the first warning cracks in our relationship began to appear. Our marriage seemed—to me, at least—to be evolving along the best possible lines. The ecstasy of the first months, too intense to last, had begun to give place to a more enduring and far deeper affection, securely based on knowledge and understanding of each other, and the intimate comradeship of shared lives. Our love for each other would continue, ever maturing and ever more satisfying, till death us did part. That was what I believed—or assumed—and certainly wanted.

It was not until the end of the fourth year of our marriage that things began to go wrong. I can't pinpoint a date. There was no sudden change, no overnight cataclysm, no dramatic rift. It was more like a process of attrition, a creeping erosion, so slow as to be barely noticeable. To change the metaphor, there was strain—not yet enough to tear the seams apart, but gradually increasing. With the advantage of hindsight—if it *is* an advantage to be made aware of error too late—I can see all the reasons for it now. At the time I could see only what appeared to be the obvious ones.

One of the most obvious was certainly not my fault—nor Laura's. She had naturally expected to start a family—hence, in part, our commodious house—but she didn't. As time went by, with nothing happening, she consulted her doctor—a local man, not Muriel—and he sent her to a gynecologist who made the usual tests, and then I submitted myself to the usual tests, and the exasperating verdict was that there was nothing to be done because there was no apparent physical reason why we shouldn't produce. It was just one of those inexplicable cases, and the advice was not to worry about it and to keep on trying—in itself, no hardship. Laura was more upset about it than I was—personally I could see very real disadvantages for a writer in having small feet pattering around the house from dawn till dusk. But of course I tried to keep such thoughts strictly to myself, and was careful not to be openly hostile when the possibility of eventual adoption was discussed.

Another source of strain was money. The books immediately following *Death at the Summit* had naturally done quite well, carried along by the earlier success, but latterly sales—and particularly the sales of subsidiary rights—had begun to fall off. I still had a big income, but the bonanza was over. At the same time the large tax demands, which I thought I had foreseen and made adequate provision for, turned out to be heavier than either I or my accountant had expected, so that the leaner years were having to pay for the fat ones. There was nothing alarming about the situation yet, and perhaps there never would be, but our expenses—lately increased by an annual allowance to my elderly parents—were high, and it worried me to see our capital being eroded. So I began to make suggestions for small economies, like cutting out some of our jaunts and eating in cheaper places and entertaining less and not buying so many new shoes and clothes. I thought it was a sensible precaution against poverty in old age, but Laura didn't see the necessity, since there was still quite a lot in the kitty. In fact she accused me of panicking. Anyway, she said, it was *I* in some ways who threw money about—and she trotted out some old grievances. Like my always paying bills the day I received them, instead of waiting for a while as other people did—though I'd explained to her that I hated owing people money, that in fact it was against my principles. We had a ridiculous set-to after one of our meals out, because I had left a generous tip on top of the service charge. I pointed out that we were known in the place and had a reputation to keep up, and that anyway I disliked appearing mean before waiters. But it didn't soothe Laura. She seemed to think I was an appeaser, trying to ingratiate myself. And she went on to develop the theme, recalling that if somebody bumped into me in a crowded street it was always I who said "Sorry!" This was probably true, but—as I told her—hardly relevant to the money problem.

One result of my slight financial anxiety was that I forced myself to work harder and faster. Writing is wearing enough even when the tempo is normal. You type till your eyes blur, your fingers stiffen, and your shoulders droop. You become so possessed by your plot and your characters that they are with you, wholly preoccupying you, day and night. You lie awake with an active mind caught in the toils of words. As far as anyone else is concerned, you're just a pain in the neck. For the time being, you've virtually dropped out of life. And that's when things are going smoothly! Now I was bashing away at the typewriter with scarcely a break, determined to get the current story finished and off to the publisher to earn some money. I cut out the quiet afternoons with Laura, and either spent the time in solitary walks, rehearsing tricky scenes and dialogue for the next chapter, or else went straight back to the study for another four-hour session. It was an exhausting daily effort, physically and mentally, and it left me irritable and intolerant. I became more than ever conscious of distracting sounds, like Laura whistling softly as she worked, or the unplanned burst of music when she switched on her transistor in the kitchen—all the more disturbing because she never seemed able to keep it properly tuned. Once, when I could bear it no longer, I rushed out in a fury and shouted, "For Christ's sake, turn that thing off." She looked at me as though I'd struck her. I apologized later, and in turn she promised to be more careful. She was very penitent, so I didn't go on about it, but it was quite a scene at the time. She did say she thought I was working too hard, but I said it was better to get the story done, and that it was nearly finished, and that after all it was for both of us, not just a self-indulgence on my part, and though I knew life was pretty dull for her at the moment, we'd just have to make the best of it.

"I'm not complaining about my life," she said. "I just wish you didn't have to be such a moody old grouch; that's all."

"You can't expect a writer not to be moody sometimes," I told her. "It's part of the job, and you should know it by now. This morning, for instance, I was working for hours on what was intended to be a very moving and pathetic scene. Would I be likely to come bouncing out, bubbling over with high spirits and laughing my head off? As Horace said, 'If you wish to draw tears from me, you must first feel pain yourself.' "

She gave a rather glum nod. "I do understand that. I really do, darling. It's just that . . . Oh, let's not talk about it any more."

It was the first open row, the first serious, upsetting row, we'd ever had. It was also the last for some time. I had made my attitude clear, and it had been accepted, and that was that. Now I could get on with the work. But, looking back—and remember that all the time I am looking back—I see that stormy morning as a sort of turning point. As with many storms, it was followed by a drop in temperature.

Instead of the warm and easy relationship of earlier days, there was now an atmosphere of constraint. Laura, who had always been so gay and cheerful and outgiving, moved tight-lipped through the house. I couldn't understand why—I certainly didn't want things to be like this. If the trouble had been no more than a lovers' quarrel, a blowing of the safety valve, it would no doubt have ended quickly in a sweet reconciliation. But there was something that went deeper—something that I couldn't fathom. Laura was brooding. She was polite, distant, cold. She was uncharacteristically silent. Silent, that is, except after we'd had a few drinks in the evening. Then she became argumentative and aggressive, picking on some attitude of mine, some critical view, perhaps, that

I'd expressed over a TV character's behavior, saying that I was always sitting in the seat of judgment, that I was really very like my father, going on about truth and honor and principles. . . . We had always had interesting and amusing discussions at dinner, amicable exchanges about everything under the sun, and very enjoyable. But now, with work so much on my mind, I wasn't in the mood for a lot of chat—particularly argumentative, resentful chat that had barbs all along the way and that didn't even keep to the point for more than a few seconds. In the past I had often laughed at Laura's lack of logic, the grasshopper way her feminine mind worked, but now it no longer seemed funny.

One thing that didn't help at all in this difficult time was an ill-advised intervention by Muriel. Seizing a moment, on one of her periodical visits, when she and I were alone, she said she thought Laura was looking very pale and peaked—which was unhappily true—and couldn't I perhaps slow down a bit and reduce the pressure? Well, as I have said, I liked Muriel, but this struck me as undue interference in my domestic and working affairs. I said, rather stiffly, that she needn't worry; I was on the last lap of the story, and no doubt Laura and I would work things out for ourselves, and soon things would be better. I had no more trouble from her. She meant well, of course, but it really wasn't her business, and I left her in no doubt what I thought.

The book was actually finished at the beginning of May. I sent the dozen or so photocopies off to my agent for distribution, thankful to see the back of it. I was completely drained. I had an almost perpetual headache, which tablets didn't seem to touch, and I had great difficulty in sleeping at night. However, I could look forward after all my exertions to rest, relaxation, and enjoyment of the bright spring sunshine. A wonderful thought!

It was just a week after the copies had gone off to my agent that Laura and I met Max Ryland.

III

The occasion was a cocktail party at the Savoy. The discerning reader will scarcely need to be told that I loathed such functions. Back in my reporting days I had been obliged to attend many of them, to mix and jostle and shout with all the rest. Now I was no longer obliged; and when the invitation came, I was greatly tempted to plead a prior engagement. Like the young Bernard Shaw, who once confessed to pacing up and down a street for half an hour before plucking up enough courage to present himself to his hostess, I was terrified of such gatherings. Hell is *they*, as a better writer than I once said. Other people always seemed so assured; I always felt so nervous. One reason was that though in my study I could hear a pin drop, in a crowd I could scarcely catch a word that was said. I would lean forward, ear cocked, with a spurious look of understanding on my face, hopefully nodding an occasional affirmative, yet having scarcely a clue what the conversation was about. I was most reluctant to go through all that again.

This party, however, was considered to be a particularly important one for me. It was being given by an American newspaper editor who had serialized one of my stories and might well want more, and my agent thought that I ought to put in at least a brief appearance. For ten thousand dollars, he said, one should be prepared to suffer. Also, there was Laura to think about. She didn't press me to accept, but I could see she was longing to go, and now that I was out of literary purdah I thought I ought to make the sacrifice. So I replied yes, thank you, and we went. The expedition got off to a shaky start, because the minicab we'd ordered arrived at Green Boughs fifteen minutes late, and I was in a hot sweat all the way to the Strand thinking about the packed crowd of celebrities who would already have gathered, and the din, and the mindless inanities I'd have to try and listen to.

In fact, things turned out much better than I'd expected. The room was large and airy with windows opening pleasantly on the river, and the company was select and reasonably small. Our host and hostess gave us a warm American welcome, and we took our drinks from a waiter and began to circulate. I stuck close to Laura who, with a little extra makeup to conceal her pallor and a smart new dress she'd bought for the occasion, looked quite stunning.

Max Ryland was one of the people we talked to. He was being practically pinned to the wall by an American female columnist wearing a large picture hat, and as we approached, I *thought* I heard her say, "Is it true that you're resting between girls?" He smiled without answering, and turned hopefully to us, and we rescued him. His face was vaguely familiar, but it wasn't until we'd exchanged names that I realized he was the popular film-and-TV actor. I'd never been much of a TV watcher myself—I was usually too occupied with the ever-fascinating world of my own imagination—but I did know a little about him. His forte was playing adventurous, swashbuckling heroes, D'Artagnan stuff, often in costume—always good clean family entertainment with a high moral tone. He wasn't a great actor, but with the sort of roles he filled he didn't need to be.

He was a very big man, a handsome blond giant, with a deep tan, white teeth, a fetching grin, and the sort of resonant voice you expect from an actor. I was trying to recall the title of the TV series he was currently in, as something to talk about, but I needn't have bothered because, to my surprise, as soon as he knew who I was, he wanted to talk about *me*. After one quick, appreciative smile at Laura, he fairly concentrated on me. It seemed that he was an enthusiastic fan of Walter Haines—not merely of *Summit*, but of some of the earlier books as well. He had really read them; he remembered their plots; he even recalled scenes he'd specially liked. It was most flattering, and Laura looked very pleased. He particularly admired a story I'd done about an oceangoing yachtsman, and the knowledge of sailing I'd shown in it, and he could hardly believe it when I told him that my personal experience of sailing had been confined to a little dinghy work when I was at university. "Mind you," he said, "if you can sail a dinghy well, you can sail anything." He was interested to know where I'd got my information, and I gave him a rundown on my nautical researches. It emerged that he was a keen yachtsman

{ 29 }

himself, and that whenever he could find the time he rushed off to a creek near Colchester on the East Coast to sail a thirty-foot sloop he kept there. He also told us he had what he called "a small shack" behind the seawall, which he sometimes used as a weekend base.

By now I'd almost forgotten that I hated cocktail parties. I was feeling quite human—and no doubt that was the impression I gave. As Laura had once told me, teasingly, I could become both sociable and agreeable when I wanted to, and people who didn't know me would go away with the completely mistaken notion that I was a pleasant fellow!

Anyway we got on so well, the three of us, that we were hardly aware of the passage of time until the company began visibly to thin. Laura and I drifted away then, and had a friendly little chat with our hosts before leaving. Ryland had already said good-bye to them, and was standing by the door. "Well," he said as we came up to him, "it really has been a quite exceptional pleasure meeting you." He regarded us in a speculative way. "Look, how about you two joining me for a sail next Sunday? The weather seems to be set fair, and the tides will be right. Maybe we could even manage a swim. I'd drive you down and bring you back. Any chance?"

My instinct at such times is always to say no first, offering whatever excuse comes to mind, and then to think about it afterward. Laura's is just the opposite. She said at once, "What a marvelous idea!" her eyes bright and eager at the prospect. Then she looked at me, and saw my hesitation—you could almost say panic—and her face fell. "But I don't know . . . My husband has been working very hard lately, finishing a book—he's rather tired." Ryland coaxed us. "Then this is just what he needs—sun and air and a change of scene. What do you say, Haines?" I wavered, and was lost. Laura clutched my arm and said, "Do let's, darling," and that was it. After all, I thought, she needed sun and air and change of scene just as much as I did, and the book *was* finished, and I *had* promised her that things would be better. So I said, "Well, it's very decent of you, Ryland, and I'm sure we'll enjoy it. We accept with pleasure."

We gave him our address and phone number, and instructions about finding us, and the arrangements were made. Ryland would pick us up at the house at nine o'clock on Sunday morning. With luck we would be at the coast by eleven, or soon after. We would have our sail, and then take lunch on board his yacht. He would be honored, he said, to have us as his guests. He sounded as though he really would be honored, and I made a mental note to present him with a signed copy of *Summit* on an early occasion.

Laura kept an unusually close watch on the barometer during the next day or two, tapping away almost every time she passed it. She was clearly looking forward very much to the weekend and was on tenterhooks lest some sudden change in the weather should disrupt our promising date. But we were in luck—if retrospectively one can call it that. The anticyclone held, and conditions grew warmer and more agreeable every day. Sunday dawned cloudless. This was going to be an English late spring day at its most perfect.

I was ready and waiting on the dot of nine, being—as I think I've indicated—rather a stickler for punctuality. Max Ryland arrived at five past nine in one of the big new XJ Jaguars, specially fitted with a roll-back top which was just right for the weather. It was exactly the sort of car I would have expected him to have. He was positively bursting with joie de vivre, his only faint concern being about whether there would be enough wind for our sail. Laura kept us hanging about for a few minutes—on these occasions she always seemed to find something that had to be done at the last moment. It was an irritating trait that I'd often commented on. This time it was an adjustment to her bikini. However, we managed to get away at last. Laura sat beside Max in the front, and I occupied the back seat. Max drove the powerful Jaguar a good deal faster than I liked, but his road sense was good, and he had swift reactions, so there were no unnerving incidents. We made good time to Colchester in spite of the Sunday traffic, and then took to minor roads and lanes, finishing up on a rough private track that ran parallel with a seawall and just below it. There were a few well-separated bungalows along the track, but only at the beginning of it. After the last one there was a gap of a couple of hundred yards or so, and then, at the very end of the track where fenced pasture barred the way, a single-story brick-and-timber chalet-type building almost concealed by flourishing bushes. I say chalet-type because at the back, where the ground sloped away, there was a wooden verandah that reminded me of Swiss mountain huts. The place was called Tamarisks, after the bushes.

As we got out of the car and approached the front door, a man and a girl appeared around a corner of the chalet. "Morning, Mr. Ryland," the man said, and the girl also said "Good morning," with a marked Irish brogue. Max introduced them—"Tim Burrows. Kathie

O'Connor"—and we all nodded hello to each other. The man was about thirty. He was tall and lean, with clean-cut, rather angular features, and eyes that seemed all the bluer by being set in a deeply weather-tanned face. He was wearing a gray jersey, a battered old yachting cap, and Wellingtons with the tops turned down below the knees. The girl was small, dimpled, and extremely attractive, with a neat figure and a gorgeous head of chestnut hair.

Tim said, "The outboard's OK now, Mr. Ryland—all it needed was a new plug. And I've fixed the water pump on the boat—I don't think it'll give you any more trouble." He glanced up at the sky. "I reckon you should have a good day."

"Do you think there'll be enough wind for a sail?" Max asked. "There's hardly a breath here."

"Oh, you'll pick up a fair breeze when you get round the point," Tim said. "About Force 3. Nice and comfortable."

"I cut the grass for you, Mr. Ryland," Kathie said. "It was getting to look like a hayfield."

Max gave her a very warm smile. "Well, thanks a lot—both of you. I don't know what I'd do without you." The pair nodded good-bye, and went slowly off together along the seawall.

Max explained. "Tim Burrows runs a one-man boat-yard about three hundred yards higher up the creek—lets out mud berths and moorings and does minor repairs. He's a splendid chap—a rugged individualist. He's been looking after my boat for a couple of years now. Kathie keeps the shack clean and the garden tidy. She works in a jam factory at Tiptree during the week, but she's happy to earn a bit on the side on Sundays. Tim's making a big play for her, wants to marry her—and I can't say I blame him—but she's not in any hurry to make up her mind. Doesn't need to be, with those looks . . . Right? Let me show you around the shack."

There was a porch in front of the door with a small wooden seat on each side. Max groped under the left-hand seat and took a key from an invisible hook. "I always leave it there," he said. "Then there's no problem for Kathie when I'm away."

He unlocked the door and ushered us in. I looked around with more than a casual interest, for I had begun to see story possibilities in the place. It was so isolated, so dramatically set beside the seawall, with the creek and, no doubt, lots of boats just over the bank, and a popular movie actor as the owner. It might well provide a good background for a book, and I was making mental notes. When preoccupied with work in progress, I could be one of the most unobservant of men, but when I needed fresh material, I had no trouble in concentrating—and I had a photographic memory for detail.

The chalet was a modest place, of no architectural merit, but it was hardly a shack. It had all the mod. cons., including mains, electricity and water—brought to it, without doubt, at enormous expense. There were two small bedrooms at the back and a sitting room at the front, on which the door by which we had entered opened directly. The sitting room was impressively large, but it was very much a weekend-holiday room— functional, but with no pretensions to elegance. One end had been fitted up as a kitchenette with sink and cupboards and drawers, stove and refrigerator, and there was a dining area close by. The furniture was of the simplest, and the floor was of stained and polished boards, bare of rugs. There was a small fireplace in one corner which at some time had been much used, to judge by the blackened chimney breast.

"It's nice," Laura said. "It's—undemanding. I like it."

"Well, it's hardly a palace," Max said, "and the plan's a bit eccentric. But it's a handy shore retreat if the weather turns bad—much more confortable than tossing about on a mooring. It's very well built, too. The chap I bought it from *was* a builder, and he put it up himself. Used good timber, good bricks, the best materials right through. Look at these door fastenings—" I examined them, and Max was right; they were lovingly done. "I guess it was his pride and joy," Max said.

As I continued to glance around, my eye lit on a set of iron dumbbells lined up against the wall. Max noticed, and gave a slightly embarrassed grin. "Got to keep fit," he said. "It's part of the job." I tried to lift the largest of the dumbbells, which was foolish. Sitting for days and weeks at a typewriter does nothing to develop the deltoids, and I could barely move it. Laura said to Max, "Come on, let's see Mr. World in action," but he just laughed and shook his head.

"Well, that's it, folks," he said. "Now how do you feel about a swim before we sail? The water should be well up the bank." Laura was all for it, and I was willing, so we fetched our things from the car, and changed, and followed Max up the sloping concrete blocks of the seawall. The scene that greeted us at the top was spectacular. The tide was high and still rising, and the broad creek with its mirrored boats lying quietly to the flood was a splendid sight. So, I must say, was Max. I had no great interest in the male body myself—the female one had always struck me as being far more attractive in every way—but on an objective view our host's sun-tanned torso was really something. His well-muscled chest looked a yard wide, and his biceps were almost as thick as my thighs. He wasn't a man I'd have wished to quarrel with.

We had quite a good swim. At least, *they* did. The water was cold, of course, at that time of year, and I called to Laura not to go out too far, for fear of cramp. She appeared not to hear me. She and Max were already well out, splashing and diving and disporting themselves like dolphins. For a while they seemed to be having some sort of race, though naturally Laura soon fell behind. I began to feel chilly after a few minutes and returned to the seawall to dry off. Very soon they joined me there, laughing and gasping. "That was gorgeous!", Laura said, shaking out her hair. And Max said, "Your wife's a wonderful swimmer, Walter—really great." Laura looked pleased at the compliment. "I'd purr if I had the breath," she said. We sat warming ourselves in the sun for a while, enjoying the placid scene. Then we went in and dressed and moved on to the next part of the program—which was getting Max's dinghy over the bank.

There was a detached brick garage beside the chalet, itself well concealed by tamarisks, and the dinghy was kept close under the garage wall. It was of fiberglass, about eight feet long, and it was resting on a wheeled trolley under a canvas tarpaulin. Max stripped off the cover, revealing an outboard motor and a pair of oars and oarlocks. I helped him wheel the boat clear of the wall—barking a shin slightly on a pile of rough wood that looked as though it had been gathered from the beach, presumably for the chalet fire. Then the three of us hauled the dinghy up and over the seawall—though I'm sure Max unaided could have done it with ease—and launched it. Max's yacht *Spindrift*, which he'd pointed out to us when we'd first climbed the bank, was riding at a mooring well out in the channel and about two hundred yards to our left. He kept it there, he told us, only during the season. Come the autumn, she would go into a marina at the head of the creek, where she'd be safe from the winter gales. It appeared there was a yacht club attached to the marina, whose burgee he flew. I listened attentively to all he said, still making mental notes.

The outboard motor started at the first pull of the cord, and we made our way—rather noisily, I thought—to *Spindrift*. I was no judge of boats, but to my inexpert eye she seemed a lovely yacht, well cared for, well equipped, and remarkably spacious for her size. Max showed us over her, as he'd shown us over the chalet, with an almost boyish pride of possession—switching on the echo sounder, uncovering the engine for my inspection, and inviting Laura to admire a set of delicate-looking china which was apparently unbreakable. This all took time. Finally he said he thought perhaps we'd better have lunch right away and do our sailing afterward, as it was already half past one. He had brought a hamper along in the dinghy and—there being no dissenting voices—he opened it up.

I don't know what classy West End emporium he'd got it from, but it left absolutely nothing to be desired. The contents were mainly gulls' eggs, Russian caviar, and lobster tails, with a couple of bottles of ice-packed Chablis and some delicious French bread, butter, and cheese. Max apologized for the absence of hard liquor, but said that as we were going to sail, it had seemed better to leave that till later in the day, when there would be no risk of anyone falling overboard! We lunched superbly, finishing up with very adequate coffee from a vacuum flask. And this delectable meal took place as we gently rocked on water the color of pearls, with the sun warming us in the cockpit and the most delicious scents coming from the shore.

Max proved an admirable host in every way. He gave his attention equally to both of us. He talked to Laura about her BBC days and the people she had met—and they discovered they had several mutual acquaintances. He pressed me to tell him about the plot of the story I'd just finished, and said he could hardly wait to read it, and that it sounded like good film material. He listened, not just courteously but with genuine interest, when we talked. He sought to entertain, and told several good stories, one of which I particularly enjoyed. It was about a bank manager. A customer went into the bank and asked to see the manager. "I'm sorry," the assistant manager said, "but Mr. Smith died last night." Next day the customer went in again and asked to see the manager. "I told you, sir, Mr. Smith has died." "I know," said the customer, "I just like to hear it." Perhaps it was the Chablis, but we laughed and laughed.

In the afternoon, pleasantly replete but not to the point of somnolence, we had our sail. The breeze was light, but sufficient. We tacked slowly against wind and tide, quietly, lazily, but still making progress; and of course with everything in our favor we did the return trip in no time at all. Max pointed out the yacht-club headquarters while we were at the head of the creek, and on the way back Tim Burrows' boatyard with its forest of short masts and the Arklike houseboat on the saltings where he lived. Max did almost all the work during the trip—tying up our dinghy to the buoy before we left, slipping the mooring, hoisting the sails, making the tacks, mooring up again. But he encouraged Laura to take the tiller for a while, patiently explaining what she was supposed to do and finally congratulating her on her aptitude, which brought a glow of pleasure to her face. There was no doubt that her day by the sea was doing her a world of good; her eyes were bright again, and the pallor of a few days ago had completely gone.

My final impression of that afternoon was that Max was a very competent man of action—off the screen, as well as on it. His sailing was like his swimming—expert. I didn't doubt that he could also ride and shoot and fish and water-ski. I admired his skills—and envied them. I would have liked to be a man of action, too.

By the time we got back to the mooring, the tide was well down, and muddy rills and gray-green saltings had emerged from the water opposite the chalet. But there was a rough causeway, an improvised "hard," which the previous owner of Tamarisks had laid with effort and enthusiasm to the half-tide mark, and we left the dinghy anchored and made our way to the seawall, barefooted, without difficulty. Max said that Tim would row the dinghy in at high water next day and return it to its place beside the garage. After we'd cleaned up, we sat around the chalet for a while, talking, and then Max produced gin and whisky, and we all had a noggin. It was nearly seven o'clock when we packed up our things, hung the door key on its hook, and set off back to London.

I had admired the Jaguar on the journey down, and did so again on the way back, and at some point Max said, "Would you like to take the wheel for a bit? It's quite an experience." I said I would, very much. Driving was one of the things I enjoyed, and that I was quite good at. I liked the feeling of controlling powerful machinery, of being in charge, of foreseeing difficulties and dangers on the road ahead—and I could sufficiently imagine the consequences of error to avoid recklessness. The Jaguar was an automatic, but so was Laura's Rover, so there was no problem. The power, of course, was marvelous, giving one a most exhilarating thrust in the back, and I very quickly got accustomed to the controls. The outcome was that I drove the rest of the way home. The trip took somewhat longer than the journey out, but no one seemed to mind.

We were all pretty tired by the time we reached the house, and Max wouldn't come in for a nightcap. We thanked him warmly for all his kindness, and said we looked forward to seeing him soon.

It had been, as Laura said, a truly memorable day.

IV

Max's generous hospitality clearly had to be returned in some degree. Even by my standards, there was an obligation. So a week or two later, Laura telephoned him and invited him to dine with us. She also asked him, tactfully, if there was anyone he'd care to bring along. We knew nothing about his "marital status"—if any—or whether he had a particular girl friend he'd like us to meet. So far we'd seen him only on his own. It had crossed my mind that he might be a queer, but Laura scoffed at the notion. "Didn't you see how he looked at that Irish girl—Kathie?" she said. "*He's* no queer!" The situation was sorted out when Max actually came to dinner. At some point in the conversation he referred to his "ex," and it emerged that he'd divorced his wife a couple of years earlier after she'd run away with a Lebanese citrus grower, a man of many hectares. "Since then," he said, with a grin that invited skepticism, "I've been interested only in my work!"

He proved as good a guest as he had been a host—considerate, forthcoming, and amusing. He was attentive to Laura, but not unduly. He was inclined to be *galant*, which she seemed to like—flattering her, complimenting her on her arrangement of flowers, on the attractive garden she had made and had shown him, on the tasty goulash she had prepared. "Jolly good!" he said, leaning back from his empty plate and looking to me for agreement.

"Not bad at all," I said.

Laura puckered her nose at me. "Walter always says 'Not bad' instead of 'Jolly good,' " she told Max.

"Is there much difference?" I asked.

"There certainly is," Laura said. " 'Not bad' is condescending. 'Jolly good' is encouraging."

Max deftly changed the subject.

We talked a good deal that evening about film-making. It was a subject that from different angles interested all of us. Max described an experience he'd had on location in the Western Highlands of Scotland. He was supposed to be marooned on a speck of an island a few miles out from Oban, and the script required him to be crouching under an umbrella in a typical Highland downpour. The unit, he said, was there for five weeks, naturally at enormous expense, waiting for this typical rain in just about the wettest part of Britain—but none fell. Every day the sky was cloudless. In the end they had had to hire the Oban fire brigade to take a float out and shoot water over the desiccated actor from the back of the island.

That really started us off. I recalled an occasion when I had invited myself to an Elstree studio—they were making a motion picture from one of my books, so it seemed fair enough, though they obviously weren't keen on having authors around—and had watched the hero and heroine at work. They were sitting on a pseudohillock in the middle of a pseudolake, supposedly engaged in a passionate love scene, and the director kept arranging and adjusting them, millimeter by millimeter. "Tilt your chin a fraction, darling. No, that's too much. Yes, that's better. Hold it. Douglas, move your hand half an inch to the left . . ." It had been love with a micrometer screw gauge.

Max said that apart from the stories I'd actually had filmed, I must have had a lot of nibbles from producers, because his recollection was that many of my books were eminently filmable. I said that motion-picture people nibbled like mice, leaving mostly debris behind. I also said that I had learned—the hard way—to have nothing to do directly with movie producers. At twelve noon they were "mad keen" on a story, and by three in the afternoon they had forgotten its name. I preferred someone else to have the coronary. Max and I had a sort of fellow feeling about this. He was on the other side of the act, but he knew the setup all right, and he said he'd done his share of suffering.

His repertoire of wholesome, slightly offbeat jokes was not yet exhausted. Whatever subject the conversation touched on—and we ranged over a very wide field—he seemed to have an appropriate one ready. We were talking, I remember, about the unnecessarily aggressive manner of a movie producer we both knew, and he came up with this anecdote—surely apocryphal. It was about a man who went to see the great Sigmund Freud and said he was suffering from an inferiority complex. Freud talked to him at some length. Finally he gave his verdict. *"You* haven't an inferiority complex, sir. You are inferior."

Another of Max's stories, a real-life one, arose out of the general mess the country seemed to be in. Some friend of his had had trouble with a gas appliance and had phoned the Gas Board for help. "We'll be around within twenty-four hours," the Gas Board had said. The friend had waited, but nothing had happened. So he'd phoned again. "You said you'd be around within twenty-four hours." The reply was indignant. "Twenty-four hours is three days for us," the GB spokesman had said. "We only work an eight-hour day, you know." I thought that was a topical gem.

It wasn't only what you might call Max's set-piece stories that enlivened our chat. He was also quick with the bright off-the-cuff phrase and the apposite illustration. We talked, for instance—it arose out of his job— about the gift of mimicry that so many actors had, their talent for mastering dialect and local mannerisms of speech. Max produced a beautiful example. An East Anglian cottager's wife had asked her husband where the yard broom was. The improbable answer came, "That stand agin the washus door that do. Do that don't that did." Max's accent was superb, staight from the heart of rural Suffolk. Then, talking about the press—another mutual source of interest—we got to discussing amusing misprints. Laura recalled one she'd liked—about someone "extending the hand of fiendship." I said it sounded like a fraternal visit from a Soviet trade-union leader. Max capped it with a professional item he'd treasured— "The mayor said, 'I have great pleasure in introducing this extinguished actress.'" Later—I imagine because there was a Test Match in progress—we got on to cricket. "Oh, cricket!" Max said. "Not for me, thank you. It's like watching celery grow." He preferred watching tennis, especially singles, which he found stirringly gladiatorial. Believe it or not, we even moved on to tombstones—the connection now escapes me, but we did—and Max quoted his favorite tombstone epitaph, which went like this:

> Here lies Jake in a lover's grave
> And sealed in a lover's coffin.
> He was a man whose wants were few,
> But they say his wants were often.

He got a round of applause for that one.

I recount all this, not to retail jokes and stories which for all I know may already have had a long secondhand life, but to give the reader some idea of the lively time we had together that evening, the pleasure Laura and I derived from Max's company, and the effort our guest made to be entertaining.

There were many more meetings with Max during that myopic spring and summer. At times he was completely tied up, shooting scenes at the TV studio or away somewhere on location, but whenever the pressure eased he got in touch with us and suggested some kind of get-together. On one of his free days he asked us to lunch at his flat. It was a splendid apartment in a luxury block overlooking Regent's Park—one of those places with thick pile carpet in the corridors and fast silent elevators and sleek cars lined up outside and uniformed porters on duty around the clock. It must have cost him the earth to live there. We had drinks on his spacious balcony high above the traffic and the treetops, and afterward he laid on a meal, with the help of an imported chef and waiter, that Epicurus would have envied. I was hardly a pauper myself, but where money was concerned, Max Ryland was obviously in an entirely different league.

We also paid another visit to the chalet—this time on a fine Saturday toward the end of June—and Max took us sailing again and gave Laura another lesson in helmsmanship, with the usual compliments of her ability and progress. When we got back to Tamarisks, he brought out garden chairs, and we relaxed on the well-shaded lawn. By now we knew each other well enough not to have to talk all the time, and replete with a good lunch, Max and Laura were soon dozing. For some reason I wasn't sleepy. It seemed a good opportunity for me to pick up a bit more local color, so I strolled off along the seawall to take a closer look at Tim Burrows' place.

Superficially it was a fairly tatty setup. The tide was out, and there was an awful lot of mud, sloping grayly to the distant channel. The boats Tim looked after—most of them small and many of them ancient—were lying in the rills at all sorts of angles; and the saltings were dotted with old engines and rusted anchors and masts on trestles and drums of oil and empty cans and bits of discarded, rotting rope. Tim's "Ark"—at once a home and a workshop—looked pretty dilapidated and much in need of a coat of paint. Yet there was something about the place that strongly appealed to me. It was, as Max had said, a place of independence, of personal struggle and effort—with not a social worker or a subsidy in sight.

Tim was there, and so was Kathie. He was scraping old varnish from a dinghy. She was sunbathing in a bikini on the saltings grass, well away from the mud, with a transistor playing pop music beside her. She didn't recognize me at first, but I recalled our first visit to Tamarisks, and her lawn cutting, and then she gave me a delightful dimpled smile. She really was a lovely girl, and I could well understand Tim's determination to get her to the church. I could also understand her own hesitation. Marrying Tim would be one thing; marrying his boatyard might seem quite another.

Tim remembered me, and stopped work for a chat. He hadn't caught my name at our first brief meeting, but when he learned that I was Walter Haines, the author of *Summit*, looking for a new background to a story and much taken with the creek as a setting, he was very ready to help. I'm afraid I pumped him shamelessly about his way of life, but he didn't seem to mind—and as far as his work was concerned, he clearly enjoyed talking about it.

He was, I soon came to realize, a most unusual man. In some respects he seemed alien to his surroundings. There was nothing of the longshoreman about him, nothing of the rustic, nothing of the rough sea dog. He was quiet in manner, and educated in speech. He gave the impression of being rather thoughtful, rather sensitive. I gathered that he had a musical bent, and played the cornet on Saturday nights in a dance band at Springford, the local village. He was a man, I felt, whom one wouldn't expect to get to know quickly. There was a hint of hidden depths beneath his amiable and serene exterior.

He told me that he hadn't originally intended to run a boatyard—he'd actually begun his working life in a solicitor's office in Colchester, and had studied with the idea of one day becoming articled. But he'd found the life too confining, he'd yearned for the sea and the saltings and the wide sky, and in the end he'd chosen freedom. Here on his patch of mud and grass he was the monarch of all he surveyed. His story, in a way, was similar to my own, except that I'd done so much better financially. His present life, of course, was tough. He was out at all hours, by night as well as day when the big tides required it, hauling on ropes, putting out anchors, recovering dinghies that had broken loose, fighting the winds and the darkness, plowing through the mud, clearing paths through winter snow and ice. It was a demanding job, calling for big reserves of will and fortitude and dedication. But he was clearly a happy man. His spare brown face showed lines of weather but not of strain; his blue eyes were untroubled by anxiety.

One day, I decided, as I strolled back to the chalet, I would put Tim in a book—and in my book, whatever the cynical reviewers might say about it afterward, he would live happily ever after with Kathie, his heart's desire.

The summer days wore on. The July weather was hot, the garden at Green Boughs a pleasant place to sit and laze and cogitate. Life seemed good—or at least a lot better than it had been earlier in the year. Laura appeared quite restored in physical health, and though she hadn't entirely recovered the buoyancy and gaiety which had been one of her great charms before our set-to, she was friendly enough and gave the impression of being reasonably happy and contented. She no longer reacted sharply to the occasional mild criticism, or deliberately provoked me into stupid arguments about trivia; on the contrary, she now tended always to agree with me, to go along placidly with anything I said or suggested, as though she had opted for the quiet life. That suited me very well. It looked as if our marriage was settling down again after its bad patch.

We were still seeing quite a bit of Max—rather more, in fact, than I would have wished. It wasn't that I didn't like and admire him; but he seemed to have become very much a part of our establishment—more so even than Muriel—and you *can* have too much even of a good friend. Also I had begun to turn over in my mind an idea for a new plot, and I wanted to concentrate on it without interruption. So when one morning Max rang up and asked if we'd care to lunch with him at the Ecu de France, I told Laura that I really was too busy—but added that if she'd like to lunch with him on her own I hadn't the slightest objection. She said, "Are you sure?" and I said yes, I was sure, and she said, well, she *would* quite like to go out, and she'd explain to Max that I was tied up with a plot. And off she flitted.

She returned around four, very bright and chirpy, with a couple of parcels. She said she'd had a jolly good lunch, and that Max had pointed out several celebrities at neighboring tables, and that afterward, she'd run into an old BBC friend, Renee Wilson, in Regent Street, which had been fun, and that she'd done a bit of shopping, and in short she'd had a very enjoyable day. Then she asked me how I'd got on.

"Oh, I think I've made a little progress," I said. "It was nice and peaceful. . . . How *is* our film hero, by the way?"

"His usual ebullient self."

"Is he still spending his Sundays down at the chalet?"

"I don't think he is," Laura said. "He's been on location the past two weekends. . . . And he's a bit peeved because he's lost the services of Tim and Kathie."

"Oh? How's that?"

"Well, Tim's just landed a big job fitting out someone's motor cruiser, and it's taking up all his time. And Kathie has decided she prefers her Sundays free after all. I guess she just wants to be with Tim. I can't say I blame her. Anyway I expect Max will soon find someone else to help him out. . . ."

I nodded, and returned to my notes.

The rest of that week was something of a social whirl for Laura. She lunched with Muriel, and the next day with the girl friend she'd met—Renee Wilson; and the day after that, she took a dress back to some shop, saying she'd decided it didn't suit her. Laura often had second thoughts about her purchases. It always baffled me that she couldn't reach a decision and stick to it, and I told her so, but all she said was that a man couldn't be expected to understand and that anyway *I* wasn't being inconvenienced. She seemed a little short-tempered, for no discernible reason.

A couple of days later, she sprang a surprise on me. We had just finished breakfast. Suddenly she said, right out of the blue, "Darling, let's go away somewhere. It's ages since we did."

"I'm willing," I said. "Where shall we go?"

"Oh, anywhere—it doesn't matter. Let's take the station wagon and drive through France—that's always fun. . . . Let's go tomorrow."

I smiled at her eagerness. "We can hardly do that," I

said. "We'd have to make some preparations. Travelers' checks and documents and things."

"I can get travelers' checks straight over the counter—I've done it before. And cars don't have to have documents any more. Our passports are okay and that's all that matters. We could drive down to Dover in the morning and cross on an afternoon boat. *Please* let's go. I do so want to." She sounded quite tensed up about it.

I said, a little irritably, "Darling, I'm quite prepared to go on a trip, but we can't do it tomorrow. I'm expecting some proofs, and I must be here to deal with them."

"They could be sent on to you—*poste restante* somewhere."

I shook my head. "Too much of a business to arrange. Also, I might have to check references, and I couldn't do that in France. . . . We could go in two or three weeks, though."

Laura's face fell. "I see . . . Oh, well, if your proofs are so important. It was just an idea. Forget it." She was behaving, I thought, like some petulant child. I couldn't understand what had got into her.

"We'll go," I said. "But later. After all, there's no special rush. . . ."

In fact, we didn't go. By the time the proofs were read and returned, Laura seemed to have lost interest. France would be hot, she said, and the roads would be crowded. I suggested alternatives—Norway, for instance—but she turned them all down. I was beginning to find her quite unpredictable. There were days when she was completely shut up in herself, when she sat for hours with an unread book on her lap, when we hardly exchanged a word. There were other days when there was a sort of suppressed excitement about her, a kind of exaltation. I found it all most disturbing.

It was early in August that I began to wonder. About Laura and Max. Even then I probably wouldn't have done so, if they'd taken a little more care, been a little more subtle. But they just didn't bother.

By now Max was on the phone almost every other day, chatting to Laura, not asking for me. And Laura was doing an amount of shopping in the West End that even by her standards could only be considered excessive. Suddenly, belatedly—God, how belatedly!—I was out of my cocoon of self-absorption and complacency. Suddenly I was suspicious. More than suspicious. Virtually certain—at least that *something* was going on. Suddenly I realized what a blind fool I had been about Max. I say "suddenly" because that is exactly how it happened. There was no twilight period. One moment I was naïve, trusting friend. The next moment I was the jealous enemy.

Of course! It was Laura whom Max had been interested in, not me. All that soft-soaping! "A wonderful book, Walter—the best you've ever written." Just a way of worming himself into the family setup! All that lavish hospitality—the yacht, the chalet, the hampers, the flat, the expensive lunches—to impress Laura, not me. All that repertoire of amusing stories—to make Laura laugh, not me. All that flattery. . . . What a technique! And for one end. Now, with awful certainty, I saw Max as he really was—a spoiled and arrogant man, conscious of his superb physique and easy charm, methodically laying the foundations for an affair with a woman who had taken his fancy. What I didn't know was just how far he'd got with her.

Though I recoiled from the prospect, I realized there would have to be a showdown.

The crisis came on a Sunday morning. Just after twelve o'clock, Max dropped in at the house uninvited. He said he'd happened to be passing! He was as friendly and affable with me as ever, but now I could see through him, and I wondered how I could ever have liked him. Now, for the first time, I saw him as an interloper in my house, an invader, a menace I had to get rid of. I made some excuse and sought out Laura. She had heard Max come in, and was fixing her face in the bedroom. I spoke to her bluntly. I said I thought she was seeing too much of Max, that he was obviously keen on her, that if he hadn't made a pass already he soon would, and that I couldn't take it any longer. We had a short, furious row. I can see Laura now, remote from me on the other side of the room. She said I was being ridiculous. I said, ridiculous or not, I wasn't going to have Max in the house any more. She looked at me as though I were a stranger. She said in that case I'd better tell him, because she certainly wasn't going to. She seemed to be daring me to do it. So I went down to the sitting room for the confrontation.

I shall never forget that last encounter with Max Ryland—or perhaps, as you read on, you might prefer to believe, that *penultimate* encounter. He was lolling back in an easy chair, pretending to read a Sunday paper—though he must have heard our raised voices upstairs. His pose was confident to the point of insolence. He could already have been the master of the house. If Laura could have seen him then, with the mask thrown aside, I am sure things would have turned out differently. It was the give-away moment, the Jekyll into Hyde. But of course she didn't see him. She knew only the Jekyll.

I was dripping with sweat and shaking like an aspen as I faced him. I struggled to find words, dignified words. Finally I got some out. I said, "I'm sorry about this, Max, but I must ask you to leave here and not get in touch with us again. I think Laura is getting too fond of you. Please go."

He rose slowly from his chair. He stood there in my sitting room, towering above me. There was no sign of any bonhomie now. He said, "I'll go when Laura tells me to go. Not until."

I felt the blood pounding in my head. I said, "This is my house, and Laura is my wife. If you don't go, I'll— I'll . . ."

"You'll *what?*" he said. He resumed his seat and took up the newspaper again, with a contemptuous glance over the top of it. "Get lost, you pathetic little man!"

I didn't know what to say. I didn't know what to do. He seemed immovable. He seemed to have taken over. It was unbelievable. It was horrible. I turned away, and went out into the garden, and sat in the summerhouse, choking with rage and humiliation. I couldn't throw him out, and I couldn't think of any way of getting rid of him. Presently I got the station wagon out and drove to a pub, because I couldn't think of anywhere else to go. I didn't drink much, but I stayed till closing time. Then I walked around aimlessly for a while—hating as I'd never hated in my life before.

When eventually I returned to the house, Max's Jaguar had gone. So had Laura's Rover. The place was locked up, and I had to let myself in with my key. In the sitting room I found a note addressed to me in Laura's hand. It said:

> Walter,
>
> I'm leaving you. I'm in love with Max, and he with me, and I'm going to live with him. He wants to marry me. I shall be asking you to divorce me, and I hope you will.
>
> I never meant this to happen—I tried hard to prevent it—but everything got out of control.
>
> I'm afraid this may seem to you a cruelly abrupt and cowardly way of telling you—just clearing off and leaving a note. But the alternative would have been bitter arguments and recriminations, painful to us both, which couldn't have changed anything. I am already Max's mistress.
>
> I'm truly sorry that our marriage failed. It began so well, but somehow the promise faded.
>
> Laura
>
> P.S. I have taken my clothes and a few personal things. I shan't be wanting anything else.

Beside the letter, Laura had left her bunch of house and garage keys. They were as final as the seal on a document.

V

I won't harrow myself again, or attempt to harrow any residual reader, by dwelling on my thoughts and emotions on that traumatic afternoon. Half a dozen words adequately convey the picture. Shock. Incredulity. Bitterness. Anger. Hatred of Max. And, more than anything, self-pity. How could she have done this to me? What had I ever done to deserve it? In turmoil and torment, I asked the question and could find no answer.

One thing I knew for certain—I couldn't bear to spend that first night alone in the shell of a house where Laura and I had lived so happily for so long. The memories were too poignant, the sense of loss too unbearable. I threw some things into a bag, drove into town, and checked in at a large and lively hotel. For once, I didn't want to be a loner. A few drinks in a well-filled bar and the constant to-ing and fro-ing of guests might help to blunt the edge of thought. It was a stupid notion, and of course it didn't work. In the end I was merely sleepless in a different place.

Tossing and turning, I spent most of that dreadful night composing versions of a letter to Laura. Telling her of my misery, pouring out my feelings, recalling the wonderful times we'd had together, imploring her to come back, saying I was willing to forgive her. This, in finished form, was going to be one of the great letters of all time. The eloquence, the passion, the sincerity, would be irresistible. But in the light of day all the versions appeared what they were—a sterile, emotional indulgence.

What I needed in this crisis of my life was someone to talk to, some close and comforting friend to whom I could unburden myself. Someone who would understand my wretchedness and share my grief. The obvious, indeed the only person—though I hadn't seen her for quite a while—was Muriel. I telephoned her at nine in the morning and managed to catch her before surgery. She didn't sound surprised to hear from me. I asked her if she could dine with me that evening, but she said it was her night to be on call, so we arranged that I should go to her flat around seven.

I was there on the dot. It was good to see her at such a time—to know that here was someone, solid and sensible, on whom I could absolutely rely. I kissed her cheek, and she poured sherry, and sat plumply down opposite me. Her manner was less appraising than it had been in the past. She looked, I thought, rather sad. Sad for me. As I'd known, I could count on her sympathy.

I said, "I expect you've been told what's happened, Muriel."

She nodded.

I waited for some comment. Muriel wasn't usually short of words. But she said nothing.

"How long have you known about Laura and Max?" I asked her.

"Oh—just a week or two."

"Have you met him?"

"Once. Laura wanted me to."

"What do you think of him?"

She shrugged. "It's early days to say, isn't it? He's very attractive, very good company. . . ." She was silent for a moment. "I'm so sorry about it, Walter. Sorry for—both of you. You *and* Laura."

I couldn't control my feelings any longer. "Oh, Muriel—*why* did she leave me? Why did she *do* it?"

Muriel looked away, as though she couldn't bear the distress in my face, the tears that welled into my eyes. "I'm not an expert on such things," she said. "I'm not a psychologist. . . ."

"You're a doctor, and a clever one. And Laura confided in you—more than in anyone else. More than in me—I know that. . . . Muriel, what went wrong?"

She hesitated. "It will hurt you if I tell you—more than you've been hurt already."

"That's impossible."

"It won't do any good, either."

"Muriel, I *must* know. Tell me."

She drew a long breath. "All right—if you insist. I'll give it to you straight, so brace yourself. What went wrong was that you turned out to be the most self-centered, inconsiderate, insensitive, overbearing, patronizing bastard that any woman could have had the misfortune to meet."

I could hardly believe my ears.

For a moment I just stared at her in shocked silence. Then I said, "You can't *mean* that, Muriel. I don't know how you can say it. It isn't true, and it isn't fair. I was always concerned for Laura. I looked after her. I watched over her. I loved her. God help me, I still do."

"You think you do," Muriel said. "But. . . . Well, there's love—and love. I once had a very wise tutor, and he said something I've never forgotten. He said the best test of real love was whether it encouraged and supported the other's sense of personal worth. Whether it gave the impression that the other person's existence, talents, and opinions were rare and precious things. People need to feel important, Walter—to someone. They need to feel admired. They need to be approved of. Even flattered."

I considered what she'd said. In spite of the psychological jargon, I took the point. Indeed, it was obvious. But I couldn't see how it applied to me. "What makes you think I didn't give Laura enough support?" I asked.

"I don't *think*," Muriel said. "I know you didn't. Laura talked to me a great deal—not grumbling, not complaining, she was very loyal—but when she was upset, things slipped out. And I pieced them together. . . . You're a neurotic, Walter. You're practically a textbook case. You feel uncertain, insecure. You're short on self-confidence, so you try to build yourself up at other people's expense. You have to have someone you can dominate, triumph over. For you, it was Laura. You deflated her; you browbeat her; you made derogatory remarks about her; you wore her down; you crushed her personality; you stifled her. . . . She can't cook very well, so you're indulgently

{ 59 }

superior—instead of lying in your teeth and complimenting her. She's only a moderately good driver, so you always take the wheel. You complain of noise and interruptions when you're working, and she has to creep about the house feeling guilty over the slightest sound she makes. When you have an argument, you tell her she's illogical and not worth listening to. You invent a financial crisis and make her feel extravagant. You take her arm across the street as though she were a child, and warn her of pitfalls in the path as though she were a blind half-wit. You complain of headaches and insomnia to get her sympathy and make her feel that in some way she's been inadequate. You say you can't bear the rigors of social life and crowds, and she feels like a frivolous butterfly every time she goes to the West End or suggests that someone come in for a drink. . . . Walter, I could go on and on and on. Life with you must have been hell. No wonder she was resentful! No wonder she left you! No wonder she thought she'd be happier with Max!"

I stared at her, absolutely shattered by her broadside.

"If that's how you see me," I said at last, "why didn't you ever tell me? Why leave it till now, when it's too late?"

"You wouldn't have listened to me," Muriel said. "On the few occasions when I did try to remonstrate with you, you became angry at once. And Laura wouldn't have wanted it. Whatever feelings she might have had about you herself, she'd have hated to hear criticism from anyone else—even from me. It would have been a case of 'How to lose friends and stop influencing people.' It's only because it is too late, because of the disaster, and because you pressed me, that I've spoken out now."

I said, "*Is* it too late?"

"I think it is, Walter. I could be wrong—but I think it is. . . . It would be different if Laura had slammed out of the house on a wild impulse after a furious quarrel with you, and gone to Max as a kind of protest. But it wasn't like that. This situation has been building up for a long time. You may think her headlong rush at the end suggests infatuation—but I think she's been in love with Max for quite a while, really in love, and the final rush only came when she'd made up her mind what to do about it. If Max is kind to her, I'd guess she's his forever. I know it's hard for you—but my advice would be to accept the situation."

That, for the moment, was the end of our talk. The phone rang, and it was an emergency, and Muriel had to dash off. And I went back to the hotel.

I sat in the lounge there, with an untouched Scotch at my elbow, mulling over what Muriel had said. Going over her list of neurotic symptoms. Even adding a few more of a similar kind, that I knew about and she didn't. Once you become your own head-shrinker, there's no end to it.

Miserably, reluctantly, I had to conclude that she'd been right about me. I could see how, little by little, I *had* eroded Laura's self-esteem. I *had* undermined her as a person. I hadn't meant to do it; I hadn't realized at the time that I *was* doing it—but I did now. On its own, any one of the things Muriel had mentioned could have been laughed off as of no importance, a bit of harmless badinage and teasing, or a minor eccentricity. But what she had done was show me a pattern—a whole system of behavior. She had opened a window on my self; she had given me insight. She had shown me the sort of man I really was. Which, not to mince words, was a pretty awful stinker.

All my life, I had concentrated on myself. Not in the sense of self-questioning, of trying to understand what made me tick. Far from it. There had been no self-examination at all. I had never asked myself, "What am I really like?" I had concentrated only on outward things—my interests, my ambitions, my achievements, my plans. I had never considered myself in relation to others. I had never thought, never once, "What effect will that remark have?" or "What effect will that action have?" On others.

So what had my "love for Laura" been? When I tried to analyze it, it amounted, in different words, to what Muriel herself had said. . . . Enjoyment of her company—*my* enjoyment. Self-congratulation on the charming wife I had acquired—pride of possession. Concern for her physical safety, health, and well-being—part of the possession. A little power, that I could exercise—this was my wife, who rightly deferred to me. Physical desire, pleasant to gratify. . . . But never for a moment had I tried to get inside her mind—her different, independent mind—and look at things as she was looking at them. Really, in fact, to *love* her. . . .

I wondered if people could change. I was sure one's nature couldn't be changed, not entirely. All the characteristics were built-in. But one's nature was a complex of qualities, good, bad, and indifferent. Knowing oneself, it should surely be possible to strengthen some, to eliminate others . . . ?

As though it mattered now! It was all too late.

VI

I stayed at the hotel for two nights and then went back to Green Boughs. It seemed, after all, the best thing to do. Loneliness was in the mind, and inescapable wherever I was.

Loneliness! The word had never meant much to me before. It was something that happened to very old people, something that good Samaritans tried to assuage in the final years. It was rarely an affliction of the young and the active. They had enough vitality and resilience to cope. To me it had been little more than an abstraction—a thing I had sometimes tried to imagine but never experienced.

Now I knew the awful reality. The room without a voice. The chair without an occupant. The dragging hours, unshared. The silence and the emptiness. The sense of being utterly abandoned. The waking in the night, with no one to reach out to. The longing and the tears. The vain regrets for things unsaid, or too much said. If only, if only. . . .

It was worse than mourning the dead, for this need not have happened. This was a desolation I had brought upon myself. . . . Five years. All gone for nothing. All dust and ashes. Nothing left. Nothing at all. Just me alone in this echoing house. . . . What happiness, what blessings, I had taken for granted! How trivial and unreasonable my ill-tempered outbursts now seemed! Now that the singing and the whistling had stopped, and there was no sound any more to disturb the writer at his work. . . .

At first I sought refuge in alcohol, the obvious anodyne. Except momentarily, it didn't help. It made me maudlin, encouraged me to weep. It dulled the pain at night, but made everything worse in the morning. It offered no way out, and in self-disgust I soon abandoned it.

There were moments when—from a safe distance—I contemplated suicide. The ultimate pain-killer, the final revenge on Fate. I even considered methods—the severed artery in the bath, the plunge from a cliff top, the bottle of pills, the dive under a bus. I recoiled from them all. It was an academic exercise, a morbid fantasy. I knew I would never have the courage. You had to be out of control, out of your mind, or in the direst physical pain, to kill yourself, and I, though utterly wretched, was sane and healthy. Death before my time was not for me. It would come soon enough.

So what was I going to do? Continual brooding would turn me into a chronic melancholic. Somehow, some time, I had to come to terms with the situation. Somehow I had to reorganize my life. At thirty-five it should be possible to make a fresh start. . . . But better, perhaps, not to force the pace. Better to get over the shock first—to take things quietly. Try not to think about the past. Attend to routine business. Answer correspondence. Carry out the routine chores. And wait for Time, the alleged great healer, to do his stuff. Preferably without his scythe. . . .

Even in the most straightforward circumstances, a marriage can't be undone without effort on someone's part. In the case of Laura and myself, the effort was unlikely to be very great, since there were no children to consider and no financial problems, and certainly no wish on my part to hold her legally against her will. However, somebody had to take the first steps about a divorce, and I didn't see why it should be me. I wasn't the one who wanted it; it was Laura—so the initiative should surely come from her. Whatever she suggested, I would fall in with. I waited a couple of weeks, expecting to hear from her or her lawyer, but no letter arrived, and in the end I phoned Muriel to see if she had any news. I bore her no grudge for her earlier outspokenness—rather the reverse. I felt she had done her best to straighten me out, and I was grateful.

"How are things going?" I asked her. "With Laura. Have you seen her?"

"I haven't seen her," Muriel said. "But I've talked to her on the phone."

"How is she?"

"She says she's very happy—and she certainly sounded it. But she *is* concerned about you. She wanted to know how you were, and what you were doing, and

{ 65 }

how you were managing. I said you were bearing up pretty well. I hope that was right."

"It was right to say it," I said.

"You don't sound too bad."

"I'm struggling. I wouldn't want to go under completely."

"Good for you."

I said, "Where are they living, Muriel? What's the position?"

"They're living at his flat. Laura's pretending to be his sister. On a visit. She didn't much care for the idea, but it seems that Max is a bit concerned for his reputation."

"What—a film actor?"

"It's the TV angle he's bothered about—the family audience. He's afraid of gossip and what it might do to his image. . . . Laura says it's just a temporary arrangement—they'll move into their own place when things are sorted out."

"You mean when she gets her divorce—and they can marry?"

"I suppose so."

"I've been expecting to hear something—from someone. But not a peep! Did Laura mention the divorce?"

"Yes, briefly. She said she'd be writing to you about it. I gather Max has been very occupied with his TV series—they haven't had a chance to discuss things properly yet."

"I wouldn't have thought there was much to discuss," I said.

Muriel made a noncommittal sound.

"Anyway, thanks for the news, Muriel—such as it is. May I keep in touch?"

"Of course," she said. "I'll expect you to."

So that was that. Muriel's forecast had been right— there had been no second thoughts. Laura and Max had settled down, at least in a sort of way, and I had to accept the fact. Hope, lingering on, would merely prolong the agony.

I made greater efforts now to fill my time. I fixed up several overdue lunches in town—with my publisher, my agent, my accountant. A good lunch could easily absorb two or three hours of the day, with traveling, and in an agreeable way. I searched out new local restaurants, places that Laura and I hadn't been to together, so there'd be no nostalgia. I went several times to the cinema, once to a theatre, and once, rewardingly, to the Wallace Collection. I dug out the addresses of old comrades from reporting days, and much to their surprise, renewed acquaintance with them. I thought of going to see my aging parents, with whom I'd sporadically kept in touch, but it seemed unkind to present myself at a time when the only news I could give them was so melancholy, so I didn't.

Work, I knew, would be the best answer to my problem. If I could once lose myself in a story, I'd be on the way to recovery. But you can't start losing yourself until you have a plot, and the idea I'd been toying with seemed thin and lifeless compared with the real-life drama I was involved in. Maybe, I thought, I could turn my bitter personal experience to account in some way. I wouldn't have to search for interesting characters. I had several ready-made—Max, Laura, Muriel, myself. Perhaps I could weave them, suitably disguised, into a murder plot. With Max, naturally, as the murderee.

But my heart wasn't in it, and I found it hard to concentrate for long. With Laura gone, I had no incentive.

There was no one to fan the vital spark, no one to try an idea out on, no one to approve or disapprove, no one close to me who gave a damn what I wrote. . . . Perhaps it would be better if I went away somewhere. Travel had always refreshed and stimulated me. It might do so again. At the worst, movement would create the illusion of occupation. And the minor anxieties inseparable from journeys would temporarily supersede the major one. If you lack a bed or a meal in a strange land, you don't reflect on the ruins of your life. Yes, I *would* take a trip. . . . The day after the decision was made I collected an armful of brochures from my travel agent and started to consider possibilities.

It was on September twenty-sixth—some six weeks after Laura had left me—that Muriel telephoned and asked if I could drop in for a drink after evening surgery. She sounded a bit agitated on the phone, which wasn't like her. She was normally a very calm person—and of course as a doctor she was trained to be calm. I wondered if she had had upsetting news about Laura. I had still received no letter, no word of a divorce—which had continued to surprise me. Perhaps Max was reneging on the marriage plan. That would figure. . . .

The truth was far more squalid.

"You won't enjoy what I'm going to tell you," Muriel said, after she'd poured us both stiff drinks, "but I thought you had a right to know. Laura and Max have broken up."

I waited. This, I sensed, was no moment for giving three cheers. There was clearly something more to come.

"You won't enjoy it," Muriel said, "because of the circumstances. It's a pretty awful story, Walter. There's no doubt Max Ryland is one of the world's outstanding bastards."

"What happened?"

"Well, briefly, Max arranged a small party at his flat—a quartet. There was some man he knew from the film world, and the man's blonde girl friend, and of course Laura. They had a meal, with drinks before, and drinks with, and drinks after, and they all got pretty high. Max kept topping up the glasses, and the night wore on. They had a stereo session, and they danced a bit with the lights turned low, and finished up on two settees—Max with the blonde, and Laura sitting with the man. Then Max started doing a bit of fumbling, and the man made a pass, and it suddenly dawned on Laura that the whole thing had been planned, and that what Max had in mind was a sexual foursome."

"Oh, my God!"

"Laura sprang up in a fury, smashed a few things, rushed into the bedroom and locked herself in. The party broke up, and the man and the girl left. Then there was a scene to end all scenes. It finished up with Max telling Laura she was a dreary little prude, and various other unpleasant things; and that he was through with her. He gave her a couple of hard slaps on the face, and pushed her out of the flat."

I groaned.

"She wandered around the streets in a dazed sort of way—you can imagine the state she was in—and presently a patrol car pulled up beside her, and a policeman asked her if she was all right, and where she was going, and in the end she made enough sense for them to put her in a taxi and send her to me. It was two o'clock in the morning when she arrived. She told me what had happened. She was sobbing; she was heartbroken. She was really beyond comfort. So I gave her a sedative and helped her into bed. . . . This was just over a week ago. I was afraid at first that she might be in for a total breakdown, but she's got guts and a tough character—*you* know that—and after a few days of resting and talking things out with me, she began to come to terms with the situation. She said she was going to try and get a job, right away. She'd left all her things at Max's flat, and couldn't face going back there, so she wrote a note to the porter authorizing me to pick them up, which I did. She left here the day before yesterday—a bit fragile, but on her own feet. And that's the story. . . . It's a sickening business—but she'll be all right in the end. You don't have to worry too much about her."

"Where is she, Muriel? Do you know?"

"I do know—but she made me promise not to tell you. So I can't."

"She doesn't want to see me?"

"Walter, be your age. Of course she doesn't want to see you. You're the very last person she'd want to see. She walked out on you; she got herself into a ghastly mess; she was humiliated beyond belief. What do you expect her to do—come crawling back to you, saying she was sorry, it was all a mistake? Allow her what's left of her pride."

I nodded slowly. "Yes—I understand. I understand that that's the position now. It couldn't be anything else. . . . But what about later, Muriel? I want her back. I think I'd be a different man if I were given another chance. Can't you see any hope?"

Muriel toyed with her glass, avoiding my eye.

"Frankly, Walter, I can't. I could be proved wrong, of course—I'm not a crystal gazer. But if I were you, I wouldn't count on picking up the pieces. Too much has happened. The scars go deeper than you think."

"What do you mean?"

She hesitated. "Well—I suppose you may as well have the whole picture. To be quite brutal, Walter, I don't think Laura respects you any more. She hasn't said so in so many words—but I'm sure she feels that you let her down as a husband. She was drifting into danger; she knew it—and she needed your help. She asked you, she implored you, to take her away. It was an SOS—but you didn't get the message. You didn't even try to find out *why* she wanted to go. You just brushed her aside—and did nothing. And in the final crisis, you did nothing. Worse than nothing—you ran away. You abandoned your wife and home to the invader. You were ineffectual and inadequate—as a husband and as a man. How can she ever respect you again after that?"

"What *could* I have done?"

"You could have given Max a punch on the nose."

"He'd have slaughtered me."

"I dare say. But it might just conceivably have saved your marriage." Muriel gave a wry smile. "Anyway, it would have been a glorious death!"

There is nothing more shaming for a man than to be called a physical coward by a woman. Especially if it's true. And in my case, of course, it *was* true.

Muriel's words had merely dragged into the open what, in my heart, I had long known. Why otherwise, during tortured night hours, would I have indulged in

{ 71 }

schoolboy fantasies after my demeaning encounter with Max—redrawing the scene as I would have liked it to be, as it would have been for any storybook hero? "Out, you bloody swine! I give you five seconds."

Then a crack on the jaw, a well-directed kick, a knuckle job to the stomach—and out he staggers, groaning. Ruefully I caress my bruised fingers. "Sorry about that, darling. Pity he didn't go quietly. I hate violence." And she rushes into my arms. Quite a scenario—in the imagination.

Reality was so different. I wasn't merely the selfish neurotic that Muriel had denounced at our first talk. I was also a man without spirit, a poltroon who'd fled the field. I hadn't stood up to Max even in words, let alone in action. If Laura now despised me, it wasn't surprising—for I despised myself.

So what was I to do? Accept the situation? The contempt? Worse—the self-contempt?

Or could there be, I wondered, some road to redemption? Some catharsis? If not in Laura's eyes, at least in my own.

I thought about it through a long, long night.

VII

~~~

By the end of the next week, since there was no longer anything to detain me in London and much to be gained by departure, I was all set to go abroad for my mental refresher. I had picked out Portugal as a good place to visit, and some eight days after my talk with Muriel—to be precise, on the evening of Friday, October fourth, dates now being important in this story—I flew to Lisbon. I spent one night there, and the next day I rented a car and drove south to the Algarve.

I had chosen Portugal partly because it was a country Laura and I had never been to together, so there would be no upsetting memories, but mainly because I had been attracted by the pictures—of sun and sand, of orange groves and almond blossom, of picturesque windmills and delicate white chimneys, of little donkey carts on otherwise empty roads. Apart from the absence of almond blossom—I was three months early for that—the place was even better than the brochures. I drifted along the southern coast road and found a delectable spot called Praia da Luz near Lagos, where I rented a small white villa for two weeks. Luz Bay was spectacularly beautiful—a scimitar of golden sand under a massive cliff, washed by a sapphire sea. There were a lot of villas around, but it was late in the season for holidaymakers, and there were no great crowds. The little fishing village of Luz was picturesque and unspoilt. The weather was perfect, the light brilliant, the sea milk-warm, the locals friendly—this was well before the revolution—and the British expatriates happy to welcome a visiting writer. There was an excellent restaurant practically on my doorstep, and a bevy of maids to do all the villa chores. As far as I was concerned, it was lotus land.

The snags, such as they were, were minor. The spoken language totally defeated me. It was so full of *shushes* that I wondered what would happen to a Portuguese eating biscuits. The mirrors in the villas were placed by little men, so that I had to crouch to shave. The roads were playgrounds for children, unused to motor cars; the scores of stray mongrels mostly had a limp. Villagers stood around in the streets, indifferent to traffic and quite immobile, so that the scene had the quality of a painting, a kind of still life. Laura would have loved it. As I did.

Though I have called it lotus land, I wasn't entirely idle in Portugal. While I was at Luz, I picked up some fascinating background material for possible future stories. No place I had visited had offered so many natural facilities for fictional crime. There was a peninsula in the extreme southwest, a stretch of myrtle-covered moorland, where Henry the Navigator had once trained his seamen. It was pockmarked with blowholes—narrow slits in the ground that angled their way steeply to the sea far below. You could sit there on the surface, quietly picnicking, and a roar would build up at your feet, culminating in an ear-splitting scream as the Atlantic rollers poured into some cavern and forced out the air. What a place that would have been for terror and mayhem—for getting rid of someone you hated . . . ! Then there were the vertical cliffs, two hundred feet high, on which Portuguese fishermen perched nonchalantly, leaning out over crumbling ledges to cast their lines into the seething depths below. What cliffs for the gentle push! Then there was the goatherd, with animals as large and rangy as small ponies, red and brown and white and very handsome, and his biblical sling. To bring the stragglers back into the flock, he had only to drop a small stone accurately at their feet. How easily he could have disposed of an approaching enemy, however formidable, however huge! The David against the Goliath . . . Nor were the blowholes and the slings the only tools to hand. There were cacti, growing along all the paths like weeds, with tough, needle-sharp spears that would pierce a man to the heart in a second if the thrust were strong. There were worse things, too—deadly scorpions, horrible creatures that reared up to fight with venomous tails, and when crushed, disintegrated into greenish pulp. Ugh! But for the professional writer of crime stories, the place was an endless source of macabre possibilities.

However, my thoughts were not solely on crime. I'll spare the reader an irrelevant travelogue—but I did explore in those two weeks every inch of the marvelous

Algarve coastline and the soaring hills behind it. If Laura had been with me—the Laura of the old days—it would have been Paradise. Even as it was, the beauty and novelty and the beneficent sun had a wonderfully healing effect on my troubled mind. My worrying, anxious mind. . . . .

I flew back to London on the afternoon of Friday, October eighteenth, just two weeks after my departure. I telephoned Muriel from the airport for the latest news of Laura, and learned that she was installed in a good job, again with the BBC but in the provinces; and that she was in fairly good shape. This was the best I could hope for, and I was relieved to hear it.

On the following Monday, I went into the West End for a haircut. As I walked along Piccadilly afterward, an *Evening Chronicle* placard caught my eye. It said FILM STAR MURDERED. I bought the paper. The film star was Max.

I cannot do better than quote the whole of the *Chronicle* report. It appeared under a huge headline—MAX RYLAND MURDERED—and under a collective by-line, FROM OUR CRIME STAFF. It read as follows:

Mr. Max Ryland, 32, the popular film and TV actor, was found murdered yesterday in the sitting room of a holiday chalet he owned at Springford Creek, near Colchester. He had been stabbed half a dozen times with an eight-inch kitchen knife, the fatal thrust being through the heart. A feature of the attack was its extreme ferocity. Three of the blows had driven clean through the body to the floorboards below, and when found, the corpse was actually pinned to the floor by the knife. The violence of the assault suggests that the murder was committed either by a homicidal maniac or by someone with a pathological hatred of the murdered man.

In addition to the stab wounds there was a minor injury to the back of Mr. Ryland's head. Two pieces of wood were found on the floor of the sitting room, one of which had traces of hair and skin adhering to it. When fitted together, these pieces formed what could have been a rudimentary weapon, some eighteen inches long. A pile of similar wood, flotsam from the beach and evidently gathered as firewood, was found stacked beside the garage, and this would appear to have been the source of the improvised club. Police are inclined to believe that Mr. Ryland was first rendered unconscious by a blow from this club, which broke in the murderer's hand, and then dispatched with the knife after he had fallen to the floor.

The body, when discovered, was beginning to show signs of decomposition, and a preliminary examination suggests that the murder took place about two weeks ago. Inquiries at Mr. Ryland's London residence—a flat in a luxury block overlooking Regent's Park—indicate that he was seen alive on the evening of Friday, October fourth. A commissionaire at the flats, Mr. Arthur Dobbs, told our reporter that he recalled Mr. Ryland coming in at about six o'clock that evening—when a few words were exchanged between them—and leaving again at around six thirty. It seems likely that Mr. Ryland drove down to Springford Creek that evening—his car, an XJ Jaguar, was found in the chalet garage—and that he was murdered soon afterward, possibly that same night.

It is understood that on Friday, October fourth, Mr. Ryland had just completed the filming of a new TV series—a sequel to his popular "Adventure Road"—and that he had told colleagues and the press that he was going to take a long break out of town. This would account for the fact that his disappearance for two weeks caused no comment or anxiety.

An intriguing feature of the case is that the body was discovered as a result of a mysterious telephone call. It appears that someone telephoned Springford police station early on Sunday morning and reported the presence of a dead man at the chalet. The informer spoke in a whisper, and it is not certain whether the caller was a man or a woman. The call was dialed and could not be traced.

The investigation is in the hands of Superintendent Frank Maude of the Murder Squad, an officer with an outstanding record for tracking down killers, and at thirty-one, possibly the youngest superintendent in the force. Speaking to reporters today, Mr. Maude said that so far the clues were few. The wooden knife handle bore no fingerprints, not even old smudged ones, so it could be assumed that the murderer had wiped it before leaving. The improvised wooden club had too rough a surface to take useful prints. The floor of the chalet, stained a dark oak color and subsequently polished, showed traces of many footmarks, most of them made by the shoes that Mr. Ryland had been wearing. Other marks suggested that someone had moved around the sitting room in stockinged feet, possibly the murderer, but the marks showed no clear pattern, and it was unlikely they would be of help in identifying the killer.

Police inquiries into this bizarre case are likely to be made more difficult by the fact that the Ryland chalet is very secluded and hidden by trees, and that other bungalows along the private track leading to it, though well occupied in summer, tend to be deserted at this time of year. Comings and goings, particularly after dark, could therefore pass unnoticed by anyone.

That was the end of the report—and very interesting I found it.

I was going to ring Muriel as soon as I got back to Green Boughs, but I was barely through the door when she rang me. She had heard about the murder on the one o'clock news, and since then, she too had read the *Chronicle* report. She said she'd been trying to get hold of me all afternoon. I asked her if she'd been in touch with Laura, and she said no. She sounded a little more disquieted than I would have expected—as though there was something more on her mind than the well-deserved death of a scoundrel.

"I've just had a visit from the police," she said.

I was startled. "Not about Max, surely?"

"Yes. A man named Superintendent Maude called— the policeman who was mentioned in the *Chronicle* article."

"Really . . . ? How on earth did he get on to you?"

"Well, he was following a trail, and he found me at the end of it. Apparently he went first to Max's flat, and talked to the porter there, checking on the *Chronicle* report about Max's coming and going on Friday, October fourth. Then he went on to ask more questions, and was told about the visit of Max's sister, and how a night porter had said she'd left in the middle of the night without any belongings and in rather a state, and how she hadn't come back, and about the note she'd sent saying I would collect her things—which had been kept because it was an authorization, and which the day man dug up from somewhere. My address wasn't on the note, but Maude had me looked up in the Medical Directory and

I'm sure I'm the only Muriel Entwisle there. And he came straight round."

"M'm—he sounds a pretty active man. . . . What did he want to know?"

"Everything I could tell him. Who this 'sister' was—and I enlightened him about that. Then why she had rushed out in the night, and why she had come to me, and who the husband was, and whether I'd met Max, and what did I know about him. It went on for ages. Maude made hardly any comments, but he listened and probed until he had the whole story. Now he knows almost as much about Laura and you and Max and me as we know ourselves. I hated going over all the personal stuff with a policeman, but of course I had no choice. Finally he asked me if I knew Laura's address, and I gave it him. I gathered he was going to look her up right away. After that, I imagine he'll want to see you. I thought I'd better prepare you."

"Well—thanks, Muriel. Not that I really need preparing. It's all very unpleasant, but I've nothing to hide."

"Of course not, but. . . ." She broke off. "Anyway, I thought I'd tell you. . . ." Somewhere in the background a child began to cry. "I've got to go now, Walter—but let's meet soon. There's so much to talk about."

"Let's do that," I said. "I'd like to hear your views on who might have done it. . . ."

VIII

First thing next morning I went out and bought copies of all the daily papers. Practically without exception, the Ryland murder was their main story—and by now the reporters had had time to gather more information than had been available to the *Chronicle*. There was also quite a lot of speculation and comment.

The *Globe* was interested in how the murderer had got into the chalet. There had been no signs, it said, that the place had been broken into. The windows had been found secured and intact by the police, and the front door—the only door—had been locked. It was possible that Mr. Ryland had admitted a visitor on the day he was murdered—though in that case the evidence of the stockinged feet was puzzling. There were also other ways in which the killer might have gained entry. As a result of local inquiries, a Mr. Tim Burrows, who ran a small boatyard in the neighborhood and had looked after Mr.

Ryland's yacht *Spindrift* for some time, had mentioned that Mr. Ryland had always left the chalet key on a hook under the porch seat, mainly for the convenience of a local girl who had gone in once a week to clean the premises. Efforts were being made to discover who else might have known of this fact. It was understood that the door key had been found in the dead man's trouser pocket, but it was too early to assess the significance of this, if any. It was possible that the murderer had put it there before letting himself out and closing the door behind him on its spring lock.

Referring to the "mysterious phone call," the *Globe* man wrote: "There are strong grounds for thinking that the call was made by the murderer, or by someone who knew about the murder—the whispering being to disguise the voice—since no one else could have been in possession of the information. The chalet, when entered by the police, was closely curtained, and no casual passer-by, however curious, could possibly have seen the body. At the moment it is difficult to suggest a motive for the call."

In the same report there was a paragraph about the murder weapon. "The knife," it said, "appears to have been one of a set which was kept in a drawer in the kitchenette, a part of the sitting room. There is no obvious reason why this knife should have been lying handy and exposed to view, and the conclusion might be that the murderer was familiar with the chalet and knew where the knives were kept."

The *Post* had some new facts and several theories about Ryland's visit. "It is likely," their reporter wrote, "that Mr. Ryland went down to Springford Creek for the purpose of organizing the seasonal lay-up of his yacht. During the winter months this was kept in a marina higher up the creek, and it seems he recently telephoned the marina to make arrangements for the lay-up, saying he would be coming down shortly—though without mentioning a date—to take the yacht in. There is nothing to show how long he intended to stay at the chalet. It is understood that he took no suitcase with him, but all the requirements for a short or a longer stay—clothes, toilet articles, and so on—were already duplicated there. There was also a wide selection of drinks, quickly available ice, and a plentiful supply of tinned and other nonperishable foods. This may explain the fact that the contents of the murdered man's stomach—or the lack of them—showed that he had not eaten for many hours before the murder. It seems possible that he traveled down on the evening of October fourth with the intention of having a meal at the chalet on arrival, and was murdered before he could do so. There were no signs of any preparations for a meal when the chalet was entered by the police, and no signs of anything but the briefest occupancy."

The *Record*, without disclosing the source of its information, had an interesting "exclusive." It said, "Several small areas of congealed blood were found under the body, but almost none around it. The small amount of bleeding could be explained by the nature of the attack. The view of the experts is that, of the many wildly delivered thrusts, it was the first by chance that pierced the heart. The other blows, some of which struck the rib cage and others passed through flesh to the boards, produced little blood, since by then the heart had stopped pumping. There is no question that Mr. Ryland was killed where his body was found. The postmortem stains on a corpse indicate to a great extent the position in which the body was lying immediately after death, and in Mr. Ryland's case these stains were fully consistent with the posture in which he was found. Additionally, three of the knife wounds—including the fatal one through the heart—corresponded exactly with knife marks in the boards below."

The *Sketch*, predictably, had gone to town on its illustrations. There was, for instance, an artist's reconstruction of the scene in the chalet sitting room, based on police information. The body was indicated by an outline, with the position of the six stab wounds marked by crosses; and it was shown as lying not very far from the door. The discovered positions of the two bits of wood that had made up the cudgel were indicated by arrows, and the knife drawer in the kitchenette correctly marked by a circle. There was also an artist's impression of the knife itself, showing a long strong blade tapering to a bayonetlike point, and a handle of rectangular section with a sloping, flattened top, just right to take the pressure of a thumb. Inset in the story, there was a photograph of the chalet taken from the seawall; another of the garage showing the stack of wood beside Max's covered dinghy; and a third, a long shot, of *Spindrift* at her mooring. Naturally, there was also a picture of Max, looking very handsome.

Well, he wasn't very handsome now!

I awaited the arrival of Superintendent Maude with equanimity. My shuffling unease in the presence of policemen, which had so hampered me in my reporting days, had long since disappeared. As an established writer of crime stories and a member of my professional association, I had met socially and chatted freely with some of the Yard's top brass. I had bought drinks for commanders and hobnobbed with many a chief superintendent. Because of my standing I had been accorded special privileges, like being taken on a tour of the famous Black Museum. I was very much *persona grata* at the Yard's Information Department, since as a writer I was known to be consistently on the side of the police, familiar with their duties and understanding of their many problems. Things had certainly changed since the days when I'd been told to "Move on." The police were now my friends, and many of them were my fans.

It was just after ten o'clock when Maude showed up at the house. He had another plainclothesman with him, a young officer with bright red hair and a pink face, whom he introduced as Sergeant Wilcox.

Maude was impressive. He was a tall, strongly built man, with glossy black hair, black bushy eyebrows, and a penetrating dark gaze. He was quiet in manner and in voice, and very deliberate in his movements, as most detectives are. I sensed big reserves of physical and mental power. He would make a good ally, I thought—and a bad enemy.

I took the two men into the sitting room and settled them in chairs, feeling that I was taking part in a scene from one of my own stories. It was all so familiar, even to Maude's first formal words.

"I'm inquiring, sir, as I dare say you know, into the death of Mr. Max Ryland."

"Yes," I said. "I read the report in the *Chronicle* yesterday."

Maude gave a slight nod. "Well, now—I've talked at length with Dr. Muriel Entwisle, whom you know, and

{ 85 }

last night I talked to your wife. The situation between the three of you and Max Ryland has been made very clear to me, and I doubt if there's any point in going over the ground again unless you particularly want to."

"I suppose you couldn't give me my wife's address?" I said.

Maude looked a little surprised. "I'm afraid I couldn't do that, sir. It's hardly in my province. . . ." He paused. "From all I've heard, your feelings towards Mr. Ryland were very far from friendly."

I said, "Considering that he stole my wife, and tried to debauch her, and then assaulted her, and then ditched her, I'd call that the understatement of the year. He was an out-and-out blackguard. His life was nasty, brutish— and too long! I loathed him."

Maude made a throat-clearing sound. "Quite so, sir. I understand your attitude very well. . . . Now I believe you were familiar with the chalet where Ryland was killed."

"I was there a couple of times, yes. My wife and I were invited down as Ryland's guests. That, of course, was earlier in the year—when I still regarded him as a friend."

"Did you happen to notice the pile of wood outside the garage?"

"Naturally. It was right beside the dinghy that we used when we went sailing."

"And you knew, I believe, that the key to the chalet was kept under the seat in the porch."

"Yes." I glanced across at Wilcox and saw that he was making notes.

"Did you know that Ryland usually went down to lay up his boat in October?"

"I knew that that was when it *was* laid up . . . Look,

{ 86 }

Superintendent, can't we cut the corners a little? I knew almost everything about the chalet and the Springford setup, and a very great deal about Ryland. Now what exactly are you driving at?"

"Well, sir, you're pretty experienced in crime matters, aren't you? You've written about these situations—you know how the investigations go. You know the form. Surely you must realize that in all the circumstances you're bound to be the obvious first suspect."

"Of killing Ryland! Superintendent, you flatter me."

"Flatter you? How so?"

"Because I wouldn't have had the nerve. God knows I'd have liked to do it—it would have given me infinite pleasure. But I wouldn't have dared. You know the size of the man. A lightweight doesn't take on a heavyweight."

"Ryland was struck down from behind with a chunk of wood," Maude said drily. "He was almost certainly taken unawares. Anyone could have done that. Even a woman."

"A woman! Surely not?"

"It might seem psychologically unlikely—but physically it would have been possible."

"What—those long thrusts to the boards that I read about?"

"The knife was sharp. The man was lying unconscious and helpless. There'd have been no great problem. . . . Certainly there'd have been none in *your* case—at any stage."

"Well, you may be right—but I can assure you I didn't do it. I'd have been scared out of my wits."

"M'm . . . Would you mind recalling for me, sir, your movements after six thirty on the evening of Friday, October fourth?"

"Why October fourth?"

"Because that would appear to be the day Ryland went to the chalet."

"Why six thirty?"

"That was the last time he is known to have been seen alive."

"Ah, yes—I remember. The porter at the flats. . . ."

Maude nodded. "You don't have to hurry over it, sir. Cast your mind back; consult your diary; work things out; take your time. I know it isn't always easy to remember one's movements, even after a few days. . . . But before I leave here, I shall need to have a full and detailed account."

"There's no problem," I told him. "As it happens, I can give you the account right away. On Friday, October fourth, I left this house around seven thirty in the evening and flew to Portugal. To recuperate after all the wretched business over my wife. . . . I'd say that lets me out. Wouldn't you?"

"It depends, sir. On your precise movements. On the details of your journey. Let's start at the beginning and go on from there. How did you leave here—by car?"

"I left by minicab, Superintendent. I'd ordered it from Reliance Motors of Cricklewood for seven thirty, and it was here pretty well on time. The driver took me straight to London Airport—I suppose we arrived there about eight o'clock. I bought a ticket to Lisbon from Lusitania Airways—I'd made a reservation by phone, so there was no problem. I think I've still got the counterfoil somewhere. We took off about eight forty-five. It was flight number—I've forgotten; I think it was 324. Anyway you'll be able to check with the airline—I expect they'll have all the particulars. Or maybe it's on the counterfoil. I spent the night at the Ritz in Lisbon—very

{ 88 }

expensive, but soothing—and next morning I hired a Hertz car at the hotel office and drove to the south coast. I rented a villa that day at a place called Praia da Luz, and was there without a break until October eighteenth, as the Portuguese maids would be able to confirm. On the eighteenth I paid my bill at the agent's office, and drove back to Lisbon. In the afternoon I flew home—and again I should have the counterfoil. Those were my movements, and I'm sure you'll have no difficulty in confirming them from start to finish."

Maude had become visibly more relaxed as my confident recital proceeded. At the end he said, in a much more friendly tone, "Well, that sounds quite an alibi, Mr. Haines."

"Up to a point, yes. I certainly couldn't have gone to the chalet and killed Ryland on the evening of October fourth, or any time in the next two weeks, because I wasn't here. . . . Theoretically I suppose I could have gone there on the Friday night or the Saturday, after I got back, and killed him then. But I didn't."

Maude shook his head. "If that had happened, the body would barely have been cold by the time we found it. Ryland was killed long before that—at least ten days before, and probably fourteen. If your story stands up—and I feel sure it will—there's no doubt whatever that you're in the clear. . . . I *would* like to see one or two of the documents you mentioned, though, if you can find them for me. Your copies of the airline tickets, your Lisbon hotel bill, your Hertz receipt, your receipt for the villa rental—in fact, anything relating to your trip. And your passport, please."

I had kept the Portugal papers together—travel costs can be a deductible tax expense for me—and I was able to produce them at once. Maude glanced at the receipts, checking the dates; gave a satisfied nod over the airline counterfoils; and picked up the passport. He thumbed through the much-stamped pages, studying the impressions. "I suppose these would be the ones," he said. "ENTRADA. SAIDA . . . The dates aren't very legible."

"They'd probably run short of ink," I said. "Portugal's a poor country."

Maude smiled. He was becoming more human by the minute. But he was still thorough. "Would you mind if I borrowed the passport, Mr. Haines? Just for a routine check." He didn't specify *what* check—but I assumed he wanted to make sure the stamps weren't a forgery. Similar checks would no doubt be made on all the other documents I'd supplied. And quite right, too.

I told him I didn't mind in the least. "As long as I can have it back in time for my next trip," I said.

"Oh, I'll only need it for a day or two . . . Have you any particular trip in mind, Mr. Haines?"

"No, no—but I like to keep on the move. It keeps one's mind off—well, other things. And I'm always looking for fresh backgrounds, you know."

"Of course. . . ." Maude got to his feet. His silent sergeant closed his notebook and rose with him. "You've picked some pretty good ones, if I may say so. I've read several of your stories—and I've enjoyed them very much."

"That's always pleasant for an author to hear," I said. "Particularly if he's a crime writer and the compliment comes from a professional. . . . Though I dare say you find my fictional policemen rather different from the real ones."

Maude gave a tolerant smile. "Well, you writers do

take a few liberties now and again—but who cares? We read for entertainment, not instruction—and any really bad *gaffe* adds to our enjoyment." He moved toward the door. "I'm glad things have turned out as they have, Mr. Haines. I confess I was a little worried to start with, and you'll understand I had to take the line I did. But I feel quite satisfied now. . . . Will you allow me to say that I sympathize with you over what's happened? From all I've gathered, Ryland was a most unpleasant piece of work."

I thanked him. "Are you a married man yourself, Superintendent?"

"I am, yes. Very happily married, I'm glad to say."

"Any family?"

"Not yet—but my wife is a lot younger than I am. We've still plenty of time."

"Well, good luck," I said. "And don't forget to let me have the passport back."

"I won't, sir." He gave me a friendly salute, and walked briskly down the drive with his sergeant.

IX

This was the first real-life murder case that I'd been personally involved in, and I awaited the next development with more than academic interest. It seemed to me very unlikely that Maude and his sleuths would remain entirely clueless for long. It isn't only the mills of God that grind slowly but exceeding small. A major police investigation has something of the same characteristics. Maude had undoubtedly been on the right lines when he'd questioned me about my knowledge of the chalet and of Max's movements—and if it hadn't been for the alibi, I could have been in some trouble. Now he'd no doubt be putting the same questions to others. Max had been the sort of man to make many secret enemies, and the police would be working hard to uncover them.

There were other aspects of the case that gave food for thought. Traces of a sort had been left by the killer, and one couldn't rule out the possibility that the forensic experts might come up with some startling miracle of science. I had just read in the papers that the path of a bullet through the air could be discovered by some sort of radioactive trail it left on the ground—and if such a thing as that was feasible, what wasn't? I considered, fancifully, a computer being programmed to produce from the faint imprint of a stockinged foot an exact description of the stocking, the place and date of its manufacture and sale, and precise details of the foot that had filled it. Which shows, I suppose, that I know little about computers! Less fanciful was the possibility that someone might after all have been in the vicinity of the seawall and the chalet when the killer was around. That a witness might come forward. Deserted places had their own special attractions, and were not always as empty as they seemed. . . . However, in the absence of any solid information, these were pretty idle reflections.

On the day after Maude's visit, I phoned Muriel again. She was free that evening, and we arranged to meet for dinner. We had much to discuss—but one thing was uppermost in my mind. Over our drinks, I asked her how Laura had taken the news of Max's murder. Muriel said that of course it had been a tremendous shock. You couldn't give yourself to a man in blind love for five weeks and then be indifferent to his violent death, even if you'd finished up by loathing him. I could see her point. But the shock, she felt sure, would be quite temporary— the effects would quickly pass. Max had struck no roots in Laura's life. I was glad to hear her say that, even though it brought no hope for myself.

Next, we turned to Maude's call on me. I told Muriel

of his initial suspicions, and how I had been able to dispose of them by producing a complete alibi.

She looked very relieved. So relieved that I said, half-jokingly, "You didn't by any chance share his suspicions, did you?"

"The thought had crossed my mind," she admitted.

"What—a timid neurotic like me! Killing a man."

"Neurotics are unpredictable," she said. "They sometimes do surprisingly reckless and audacious things. It's a way of making themselves feel tough and masculine."

I let that pass. "Anyway you knew I was in Portugal."

"I knew you were going, but I couldn't remember exactly when. . . . So that's one person written off Maude's list."

"List? I didn't know he had a list."

"Oh, yes. At the moment, I'm heading it!"

I gaped at her. "You mean he suspects *you*. Of killing Max . . . ! He must be out of his mind."

"I wouldn't say he 'suspects' me; no—that would be going much too far. But I'm certainly under scrutiny. He came to see me again this afternoon. He wanted to know where I spent the murder weekend, and whether I could account for my time. . . . Unlike you, I couldn't produce an alibi."

"Why—where were you?"

"I was in Ipswich. I went there on the Thursday for a two-day medical conference—there were sessions on Thursday afternoon, Friday morning, and Friday afternoon—and as the weather was pleasant and I'd never seen the town, I stayed over till Saturday. I could easily have gone to Springford on the Friday evening—I had my car with me, and it's only about half an hour's drive from Ipswich. I can't prove that I didn't, and I shouldn't think anyone else would be able to. I was staying in a busy hotel, with lots of comings and goings, and I didn't eat till nearly nine, so there's a gap of several hours that no one can vouch for. I was actually reading in my room for much of the time—but there's only my word for it."

I said, "But it's ridiculous, Muriel. You don't fit the scene at all. You weren't even familiar with the chalet."

"I'd never been there—but I'd had a pretty detailed description from Laura. I knew where it was, what it looked like, and more or less how to get there. I could certainly have found it if I'd wanted to . . . . Laura had even mentioned about the key being kept on the hook— she thought it was rather silly, because it could have become known locally and anyone could have walked in and burgled the place. . . . So I was quite well informed."

"Maybe. But you couldn't possibly have known that Max was going to be there that weekend."

"True—but I think Maude was toying with the idea that I might have gone there on a sort of reconnaissance, as I was fairly close by—and that Max happened to turn up."

I gave a derisive snort. "Of all the unlikely things . . . ! Anyway, it's fantastic to suppose you'd clobber Max with a chunk of wood and then stab him to death. It's—it's lunacy."

"Well, I'm large enough for a bit of clobbering. And I've a pretty good nerve, or I wouldn't be a doctor. I had plenty of motive—the same as yours, and almost as strong. Plain bloody hatred of the guy! I *could* have done it, you know."

"But you didn't."

"No." Muriel smiled. "Someone else got in first!"

"Then you've nothing to worry about."

"Oh, I'm not worried—not more than anyone would be who was being checked over by the police. I'm just interested in Maude's approach. He's obviously going to turn every stone."

"Is there anyone else on his list?"

"Well—Laura, of course."

"*Laura!*"

"Why not? Once you're prepared to accept that the killer could have been a woman, she's a natural. She's living not a thousand miles from Springford; she knew everything about the chalet; she knew Max often went down there at weekends; she's got her car with her—and heaven knows she had a motive. I only hope she can account for her time better than I could. I believe Maude's seeing her again this evening."

"Well, I think he's absolutely crazy. Laura would barely have reached to Max's shoulder. Can *you* imagine her doing what was done?"

"*I* can't," Muriel said. "But apparently Maude can. 'Hell knows no fury like a woman scorned,' and all that. To do him justice, I think he's only going through the motions. He's a very methodical man. He's also a very intelligent one. My guess is he'll sort things out—and I certainly wouldn't want to be against him at the crunch."

I knew what she meant. Hadn't I had the same feeling myself?

On the whole, I would say that the press and TV men gave us very little trouble during the days that followed the uncovering of Ryland's murder. Naturally they were concerned with all the facets of the story—and the facets did include myself and Laura and—indirectly—Muriel. For a short time the reporters swarmed, besieging our residences and firing their spiky questions. But because I had once been in the same line of business, I knew what to do. Of total silence, they could make nothing without the grossest invention. When they came to me, I said, "Gentlemen, I have nothing whatever to say—and I shan't have anything to say. So you might just as well go away." And in the end, by ones and twos, they went away. I advised Muriel, and they went away from her, too. Muriel, in turn, advised Laura, in case they found out where she was living (which they did)—and in turn she had nothing to say. Finally they all departed. The moral? If you are involved in a sensational case and don't want to bare your soul, consult an ex-reporter. The thing is to keep your trap firmly shut. How well, from experience, I knew it . . . !

None of this meant, of course, that I wasn't interested in what the press was saying about the murder. During the couple of days that followed the discovery of Max's body, I listened constantly to broadcasts and read every London paper I could lay my hands on. I was anxious not to miss any new development—though in fact there seemed little to miss. Maude was reported to be conducting a number of interviews in various parts of the country, but no names were given. Now that particular individuals were involved in his inquiries, he was being very unforthcoming. The post-mortem findings on Ryland confirmed what had previously been suggested—that he had been killed instantly by a blow through the heart, and that the subsequent stabbings had been superfluous. And that was about all. However, the murder was still a front-page story in the national dailies, and the paucity of matter didn't deter the crime reporters and feature writers from doing "think pieces," and rehashing the facts that had already appeared in print.

The only paper to break new ground was a rather unpleasant little tabloid called the *Star*. It published one of those articles that the less reputable newspapers are so fond of—debunking a popular favorite once he's dead and there's no longer any risk of a libel action. Not that, in this particular case, I had any objection to the debunking. The line was that Max Ryland, the pure and chivalrous Galahad of the small screen, so admired by parents and children alike, had not been the knight in shining armor that his fans had imagined. The regrettable truth, the article said, was that he had had his share of mortal failings, one of them being to exploit his good looks and splendid physique with any attractive girl he came across. He had not, in fact, been a hero on horseback but a lecherous prancing goat. No names were mentioned, the victims being still alive, but some fairly succulent details were given about the experiences of Miss A. and Miss B. and Mrs. C. in various parts of the world. Only considerations of space, it was indicated, prevented the pursuit of the subject to the end of the alphabet! Nothing in this surprised me. A man who could behave as Max had behaved over Laura was unlikely to have had scruples over other women. The final bit of information in the article was in line with all the rest. It appeared that Ryland had been married twice, both times in his twenties. His second wife had divorced him—not, as he'd said, the other way round—and his first wife had died from an overdose of barbiturates.

The article strengthened my belief that there must be many people around who had had unfriendly feelings about the late Max Ryland. It looked as though Superintendent Maude was going to have a busy time, turning all the stones.

How wrong I was!

Three days after his first visit, Maude called again at Green Boughs. This time he had telephoned in advance to ask if the call would be convenient, and he arrived without his note-taking sergeant, which showed how things had changed in my favor. I offered him a glass of sherry, and—contrary to what I had so often written about policemen never taking a drink while on duty—he accepted with alacrity. He even raised his glass to me. "Here's to more good plots, Mr. Haines." He couldn't have been friendlier.

"So what's the position?" I asked when we were seated.

"Well," he said, "we've checked over all your information, from Reliance Motors onward. There are no problems at all." He produced the various documents I had given him, and passed them to me. He also handed over my passport. "Thank you for the loan. Again, there are no problems."

"Then I can take it," I said, "that I've been—what's the phrase?—'eliminated from the case.'"

"Absolutely. I'm sorry there was ever any question, but I'm sure you appreciate that in these matters we can't take anything for granted."

"Yes, of course. . . . By the way, I gather you've been interviewing Dr. Entwisle and my wife again—and in a rather pointed fashion. I must say I was surprised about that. . . . What's the position there?"

"It was pure routine, Mr. Haines. I had to do it—but I never seriously believed that either of them was involved. Now, for good reasons, I'm sure they weren't."

"So they're eliminated, too?"

"Yes, indeed. I shan't be troubling them again."

"Well," I said, much relieved, "that's quite a clearance."

Maude nodded and sat back, very relaxed. "Now that we're on the same side, so to speak, there's something I'd be glad to have your view about. We've been making quite extensive inquiries in the Springford area during the past day or two, and something interesting has come up. Do you know a man named Tim Burrows?"

"The boatyard man. Yes, I do. Not well—but I've talked to him at some length. He used to look after Ryland's yacht."

"That's right. . . . Tell me, what do you think of him?"

"I think he's a splendid fellow. Hard-working, tough, independent. I admire him."

"Intelligent, too, would you say?"

"Very much so. I believe he was doing quite well in a solicitor's office before he got the urge to work for himself."

"Was he? I didn't know that. . . . A fairly sharp young man, in fact."

I frowned. " 'Sharp' sounds a little derogatory, Superintendent. I prefer 'intelligent.' . . . He's certainly an unusual man to find working in the mud beside a seawall. He seemed to me to have some of the qualities of an artist. Sensitivity—imagination . . . I must say I quite took to him."

Maude gave a noncommittal grunt. "Did you meet his girl friend, Kathie O'Connor?"

"Yes, briefly. Quite an eyeful, I thought."

"She certainly is," Maude agreed. "But she's not his girl friend any more."

"Oh, dear. I'm sorry to hear that. What happened?"

"Ryland seduced her."

"*No!*"

"It's a fact. We picked up some gossip, mainly in the local pub. You know how things get around in these small country places—everyone knows everything. Sometimes the rumors aren't true, naturally—but this one was. I asked Burrows about it, and he told me. I saw Kathie, too. She's moved away—she's working in Chelmsford now. She filled in the picture—reluctantly, of course. It wasn't a pretty one."

So that, I thought, was why Tim and Kathie had suddenly stopped working for Ryland. The explanation he'd given to Laura had been sheer invention. I felt very depressed. "Poor kid," I said. "Poor Tim."

Maude nodded. "It happened on a Sunday, early in July. You know Kathie used to go and clean Ryland's chalet on Sundays?"

"Yes."

"Well, she was busy there when Ryland showed up. Burrows was away at Maldon, collecting a boat. Ryland laid on the charm, chatted the girl up. I don't need to tell *you* how attractive he could be to women. Naturally she was flattered—this dazzling hero of the screen, taking a personal interest in *her*. She's a simple, inexperienced girl—young for her eighteen years and with little knowledge of the world. Anyway, he persuaded her to have a drink with him, then another. Gin, I gather. She wasn't used to it. In the end she hardly knew what happened. It must have been damn nearly rape."

"And she told Tim!"

"Not just like that. But she was so upset and miserable that in the end it all came out. She tried to avoid Burrows at first, but of course that didn't work. He kept at her, wanting to know the reason, and finally she broke down and blurted it all out. And that was the end of their romance."

"Did Tim break it up?"

"No—I gather *she* did. She was ashamed. She just cleared off."

"Well," I said, "I couldn't be more sorry. . . ." Until now, the larger implications of the story had escaped me. I had been too concerned with the melancholy facts, too horrified at the revelation. Now, with Maude's questioning gaze upon me, I realized there was more to come.

"Burrows," he said, "didn't strike me as the sort of man to take no action in a situation like that. What would you say, Mr. Haines?"

I was reluctant to say anything—but silence wouldn't have helped. So I stalled. "Is there any reason to suppose he took action?"

"We're pretty sure he took *some* action," Maude said. "This is local gossip again—but it seems that for a few days back in July, Burrows was walking around with a black eye and a cut lip. His story was that he'd slipped off a cabin roof while he was working—and that's what he told me when I asked him about it. The locals have the idea that he squared up to Ryland at some point, and took a beating."

"But he denies it?"

"Yes."

"It would have taken a lot of guts. He's a well-built chap, but he wouldn't have had a chance against Ryland."

"I'd say he *has* a lot of guts. I gathered that that was your view, too."

"Yes. . . ." There was a moment of silence between us. Then I said, "I assume you're now going on to suggest, Superintendent, that Tim Burrows killed Ryland?"

"He certainly had a strong motive."

"So had I—but I didn't do it. Motive alone isn't enough. Is there any solid evidence against him?"

"There's no material evidence—but there's a circumstantial case. He was familiar with the chalet. He'd have known about the pile of wood. He'd have known where the knives were kept. He knew where the chalet key was hidden, and could have let himself in at any time. He had a close working arrangement with the yacht marina, and would probably have heard that Ryland was due to come down for the lay-up of his boat. The furious stabbings would have been in line with his feelings about Ryland . . . What's more, on the evening of October fourth he took a walk along the seawall in the direction of the chalet."

"He admitted that!"

"Worse, Mr. Haines—he denied it. He said he was in his houseboat all the evening. But he was unlucky. He happened to have been seen by a local couple who were necking on the bank."

"Oh, lord . . . ! How did he explain his denial?"

"He said everyone in the district knew there'd been trouble over Kathie, and that Ryland had been the cause of it, and that he was afraid he'd be suspected of Ryland's murder."

"It sounds a fair enough explanation to me. One defensive lie doesn't make a man guilty."

"Perhaps not—but it certainly doesn't help his cause. And the fact remains that Burrows *did* walk toward the chalet at what appears to have been the crucial time. So he had opportunity, motive, all the necessary knowledge. And there's no one else in sight who begins to fill the bill."

I couldn't let that pass without protest. "Maybe not in sight," I said. "But that could merely mean that no one else has yet been uncovered. I dare say you read that piece in the *Star*—about Ryland's record as a womanizer. There must be many people with a perfectly good motive for killing him. Friends, relatives, of the girls. Or of the wife who committed suicide. . . . As for knowledge and opportunity, Tim isn't necessarily unique. What about the people at the yacht club? How can you be sure Ryland wasn't messing about with some member's wife? Any of those chaps could have been familiar with the chalet set-up, and Ryland's movements."

Maude shook his head. "I naturally thought of the yacht club. I've had a squad of men working on the members and the staff for the past three days. The view was unanimous. Nobody had heard the tiniest breath of scandal about Ryland until the Kathie story broke. On his rare visits to the club his behavior had always been impeccable. . . . As for the scattering of girls mentioned in the *Star*, what would they—*or* their friends and relatives—have known of Springford, of the pile of wood, of the key under the seat, of the knives in the drawer, of Ryland's day-to-day movements? I'm not ruling out the exceptional possibility, the thousand-to-one chance—but I have to look at the thing reasonably, and my reasonable conclusion remains—that there's no one but Burrows in sight. . . . Anyhow, we shall see."

I could think of nothing more to say on Tim's behalf. "So what are you going to do about him?" I asked.

"He's already been taken in for further questioning," Maude said. "I'm pretty sure he's our man—and I think we'll get the truth from him. I'd say the Ryland case is virtually closed."

X

The hours that followed that second visit by Maude were, I suppose, the real turning point of my life.

His disclosures had shaken me to the depths. I had never imagined for a moment that Tim might become a suspect in the Ryland case. Now that he had, I couldn't blind myself to the very great danger he was in. Short of being caught red-handed on the job, he could hardly have faced a more damning set of facts. This, despite what I had said to Maude, was my private view. Even on the evidence so far, he might well be charged with the murder—and convicted. And he faced this fearful danger alone. My sentimental hopes of a happy-ever-after for him and Kathie had come to nothing. Ryland had messed up their lives, as he'd messed up mine. In all this tragic business, Ryland was the only real villain. His death, I believed, had been a just execution rather than a murder.

. . .

I sat for long hours, barely aware of the passage of time, worrying, pondering, heart-searching. Thinking about Ryland and Kathie and Tim; about myself and Laura; about law and right and conscience; about killing and justification; about jail and punishment; about selfish neurotics and the path to redemption. And about many other things. . . .

I won't pretend it was easy for me to take the decision I did. One draws back instinctively from a precipice. I was well aware what the likely—perhaps the inevitable—consequences would be for me. It would be so simple to say nothing at all, to do nothing at all, to let things take their course. So simple—yet, in the light of my knowledge, so weak, so contemptible. . . .

In the end, after a day and a night of mental stress and intense mental activity, I had absolutely no doubt what I must do. . . .

At ten o'clock next morning I began a search by telephone for Superintendent Maude. As usual, he was on the move, and I had great difficulty in tracking him down. However, with the help of the Colchester police and a slice of luck, I finally managed to catch him around one o'clock at his temporary Springford headquarters. He seemed a little surprised to hear from me.

I said, "Superintendent, I have something of the greatest importance and urgency to tell you about the murder of Max Ryland. It is far more urgent than anything you can conceivably be doing at the moment. Will you please come and see me at once, with your sergeant and a tape recorder."

I don't suppose Maude had ever received a message

like that in his life before. Certainly not, in such peremptory terms, from a mere citizen. Still, I had become in a semiprofessional way his collaborator, a man whose judgment over crime matters he respected, and he remained courteous. He said, "Can't you tell me on the telephone what it's about, sir?"

"No," I said. "This is something that will take several hours to tell."

He hesitated—but only for a moment. I heard him speaking to some colleague. Then he said, "Very well, Mr. Haines. We'll be with you as soon as we can."

They must have left Springford almost at once, because in spite of the two-hour drive they arrived at Green Boughs before three o'clock. Maude didn't look any too pleased as I led the way into the sitting room. He said, "I hope this really is urgent, Mr. Haines. If it had been anyone but you, I'd have asked a local officer to call."

"You won't be sorry you came," I told him. "I'm about to clear up your case for you. Would your sergeant please start his recording machine?"

Maude gave a curt instruction to Wilcox. "Well," he said, "what's it all about?"

"I wanted to tell you, Superintendent, that in Tim Burrows you've picked on the wrong man. I know he didn't kill Ryland."

"Oh? *How* do you know?"

"Because *I* killed him. You've forced me to admit it by making out your case against Tim. Nothing else would have done so. But whatever the consequences to myself, I can't let an innocent man suffer for my actions— particularly a man I admire and respect. I'd never sleep at night again."

For a moment, Maude stared at me in astonishment.

Then, in a tone of extreme annoyance, he said, "What are you up to, sir? What's the game? You couldn't possibly have killed Ryland. We've been into all that. When he was killed, you couldn't have been anywhere near the chalet. You were either on your way to Portugal or already there. We know this for a fact. We checked and rechecked every detail. It would have been a physical impossibility for you to have been at Springford. So I repeat—what's the game?"

I said, "If Mahomet can't get to the mountain, Superintendent, the mountain has to come to Mahomet."

He gave me a black look. "I'm not in the mood for riddles, sir. You didn't, I take it, have the chalet transported here for an hour!"

"Believe it or not," I said, "you're surprisingly close to the mark. In a sense, that's exactly what I did do."

His dark eyes scoured me. "I don't get you, sir."

"Then let me explain." I motioned him to a chair and sat down opposite him.

What follows, give or take a few words, is what I told him. Walter Haines's confession. . . .

XI

~~~~~

"You will readily understand, Superintendent, how I felt
after Max Ryland had humiliated me in my own house
and taken my wife, Laura, away from me. I would never
have imagined myself capable of such visceral hatred—
but I discovered I was. Given the opportunity, I would
gladly have killed him. What I mean is that I *felt* like
killing him. But, practical considerations apart, I still had
hopes that Laura would return to me one day, disillu-
sioned and repentant, and I realized that killing her lover
while she was still infatuated with him was hardly the
best way to get her back into my arms. So all I could do
was nurse my hatred, and await developments.

"As you know, they weren't long in coming—and after
Ryland had thrown Laura out, the situation was quite
different. Killing him would no longer have any effect on
my relations with her, then or in the future. She had not
only finished with him—she had also, Muriel Entwisle

told me, finished with me. She despised me, Muriel said, for my cowardly behaviour, for my weakness as a man and a husband, and there could never be a reconciliation. That left me free to take revenge on Ryland, if I could. I had little else to occupy me, and thought of revenge helped to fill the great gap that had been torn in my life.

"There were two main problems. The first was that in the event of Ryland's murder I was virtually certain to come under suspicion and be closely questioned. Apart from Laura herself, I was the person who had suffered most at his hands—and I had never attempted to disguise my feelings about him. Undoubtedly I would be the prime suspect. So unless I could produce an absolutely cast-iron alibi, I would be in grave danger. And a long term of imprisonment seemed too high a price to pay even for the pleasure of getting rid of that unspeakable man.

"The second problem was just as difficult. I was *afraid* of Ryland—of his strength and size—and I could think of no safe way of killing him. An open physical assault was out of the question—it would have been like tackling a tiger with your bare hands. And, in common with the maiden ladies and scholarly old gentlemen who provide so many of our crime stories, I had no personal experience of the weapons my characters so skillfully employed. I knew nothing of guns, except on a purely theoretical basis. I had never used one, nor even handled one. In any case, I wouldn't have known how to get hold of one—and if, somehow, I'd managed to, there'd still have been the danger that it would be traced back to me. So guns were out. I considered poison, but only briefly. After the total breach between Ryland and myself, it wasn't likely that I would ever have the opportunity of dropping cyanide into his whisky during a social chat. No doubt I could have got hold of some poison without signing a register—I'd written enough about the dangers lurking in the hedgerows—but if I couldn't administer it, there was no point. So that was out, too. And I couldn't see myself organizing a staged accident. I had never been convinced by the comparative ease with which film gangsters ran down their fleeing enemies on pavements. My method, if I could find one, would have to be much more simple and certain.

"Well, I dwelt upon these twin problems almost incessantly, by day and night. You may think that an exaggeration, Superintendent, but as I say, with Laura gone I had little else to occupy me. What I did was to attack the problems as though they were difficulties that had cropped up in a story plot—difficulties that by ingenuity and inventiveness and sheer persistence could eventually be overcome. And in the end I overcame them both, as you shall hear.

"Working out a watertight alibi was in fact quite pleasurable. It was not only a relief from tedium—it was a stimulating challenge, an intellectual and technical exercise which I enjoyed. In its final form it was so audacious, so complex, and yet—if the logistics went well—so certain of success, that I regarded it as one of my outstanding professional triumphs. I was almost sorry to have to use it in real life, rather than in a story.

"Settling on the actual method of murder was less enjoyable. I could see that if it was to work in with the alibi—and it had to—some violence, some blood, was inescapable. Back in my reporting days I had to some extent overcome my natural squeamishness about blood—but that had been a long time ago, and anyway I had never been responsible for the flow. Now I would be—and I had to steel myself to the prospect. Wakeful in the early hours, I could hardly bear the thought. As Bonaparte once said, Three-o'clock-in-the-morning courage is a rare thing—and I certainly had none. But in daylight my nerve and will recovered. By constantly envisaging the prospective scene, by imagining the blow being struck, the knife penetrating the flesh, the blood spurting out, the prostrate corpse, I hardened myself for the deed.

"The action began with a reconnaissance. I had a pretty good general recollection of the chalet and its facilities, having thought of them as part of a possible background for a story, but there was a detail I had to check before I could lay—or perhaps I should say, remove!— the foundations of my plan. One night shortly before October fourth, I drove down to Springford with a torch and a pair of rubber gloves in my pocket and, hopefully, a bag of tools in the back of the station wagon. There were no lights showing in any of the bungalows along the track; there were no other cars around; there was no sight or sound of anyone at the chalet. As I'd expected, I had the whole place to myself. I parked the car among the tamarisks, took the tool bag into the porch, slipped off my shoes, drew on the rubber gloves, groped under the seat for the key, and let myself in, closing the door behind me. I made sure the curtains were fully drawn over the windows in the sitting room. Then I started to examine the floorboards by the light of the torch.

"This was the critical moment of my 'reco.' If the boards had been nailed to the joints in the usual way, I would have been faced with the problem—not perhaps insuperable, but certainly tricky—of getting the nails out and prising the boards up without leaving any obvious traces. I'm not sure that I would have risked it. However, I was in luck—luck, I may say, that wasn't entirely unforeseen. Ryland had told me on my first visit that the former owner had built the chalet with loving care and attention to detail, even going so far as to use brass screws instead of nails for all the fastenings in order to avoid corrosion from the salt sea air. And this was precisely what he had done with the floorboards. Nothing could have suited me better. Whereas, by now, iron nails would probably have rusted in, these brass screws would come out with comparative ease. I was ready to start work.

"I stood back, eyeing the boards. They were about nine inches wide, and were laid across the joists in eight-foot lengths. They were in excellent condition, and were set very close together, so that there were no visible gaps between them. I chose four boards not too far from the door, selected a screwdriver of the right size and power, arranged the torch on the tool bag so that it shone down on the working area, and—using the greatest care in order not to make any scratches on the heads—removed the screws. There were sixteen of them, two to each board at each end, and the job took about half an hour. When I'd finished, I wrapped the screws in a handkerchief and put them in a jacket pocket. Then I eased up the boards and leaned them side by side against the wall near the door.

"Next I padded over to the kitchenette, to the drawer where Ryland kept his kitchen knives. I knew they were there, and what they were like, because he'd proudly shown them to Laura on our first visit. By the light of the torch I picked out one with a long, strong blade, a good handle, and a point like a sword, and put it in the tool bag.

"That completed my inside work—but there was still much to be done outside. I switched off the torch, opened the door, and carried the floorboards one by one to the station wagon, placing them carefully so that they would suffer no damage, and in the order in which I had taken them up. I was still in stockinged feet. I knew there might well be old shoe marks of mine around the chalet, but I wanted to avoid leaving too many fresh ones. I made a final journey for the tool bag, closed the chalet door behind me on its spring lock, and put the key in my pocket with the screws. It seemed very unlikely that anyone would come to Tamarisks in the next couple of days—Ryland, I knew, was busy filming—but with the planks removed and a gaping hole in the floor it seemed a sensible precaution.

I picked up my shoes and went round to the side of the garage. The only sound was the occasional squawk of a seabird and the gentle lapping of waves beyond the wall. My torch was now showing hardly more than a glimmer, but there was reflected light from the sky, and I was able to select from the heap of flotsam a piece of wood that felt as though it would make a good cudgel. I put it with the tool bag in the station wagon and returned to the garage. I was trying to be very methodical about everything. I heaved the outboard dinghy off its light, wheeled trailer, and carried the trailer to the car and shoved it in the back, tying it up so that it couldn't bang or scratch the floorboards. I hauled the dinghy back in place against the garage wall, collected my shoes, put them on—and that was it. I drove home—with floorboards, screws, cudgel, knife, and trailer. This is what I meant, Superintendent, about the mountain coming to Mahomet. . . .

"On the Thursday preceding Friday, October fourth, I made some more preparations, this time at home. As I mentioned earlier, I had stowed the floorboards in the station wagon in the order in which I had taken them up—starting from the door side of the chalet sitting room. The reason for this was that in case of any slight warping or irregularity in any of the boards, I would know that I could still fit them together perfectly, because in the same order they'd fitted perfectly before. Now, working quietly in my big garage behind closed doors, I screwed light battens across the four boards, one at each end, which kept them tightly together and helped to form a rigid structure. I now had a sort of stretcher, eight feet long and about three feet wide, which could comfortably accommodate a man. I placed it lengthways along the inside of the garage wall, together with the dinghy trolley, and covered both with an old sheet of balloon cloth I had once used to protect a car from the weather. I also concealed the knife and the cudgel there. Naturally I wore gloves for these and all subsequent operations.

"The morning of Friday the fourth was also a busy time. This was the day for what I hoped would be my final preparations. I got out my working overalls, which I hadn't worn for some months, and placed them handily on a kitchen chair. I searched for and found a large plastic groundsheet, which in the old days Laura and I had found useful for picnics when the grass was damp. I spread this out on the lawn behind the garage, and put the improvised stretcher on top of it. As the lawn wasn't overlooked, and there was no way through to the garden except via the house or the garage, nobody would see it. I picked out a couple of stout eight-foot planks, left over from timber I'd ordered but hadn't needed, and placed them in readiness against the garage wall. I also put the cudgel in the spot I had chosen. Finally I reversed the position of the station wagon in the garage, so that the back of it was close to the big rear door that opened into the garden. In the afternoon I tidied up the house, and packed a bag for my projected trip to Portugal.

"I was now as ready as I ever would be to deal with Ryland. I had reached the point, I knew, at which my careful plans could easily come unstuck. Ryland might be out of town—though I didn't think so, because I'd read that every day in a gossip column that the shooting of his new TV series was in the last stages at a London studio. Alternatively, he might have a date for that evening, and be unavailable at his flat. Naturally I'd foreseen the possibility. It didn't worry me unduly. The next day, or the next, would do almost as well for me. I wasn't committed to any time schedule. I had made my airline reservation, but if necessary I could be a no-show. I hadn't burned any boats. All I had done so far was purloin a few floorboards. If I had to, I could safely wait.

"The major problem, of course—and I had given it a great deal of thought—was how to get Ryland to come along to the house at all. Considering the way he had treated Laura and myself, he would hardly be eager to pay me a visit, whatever my pretext for inviting him. However, I had a plan—and I felt there was more than a chance that it would work. Ryland, I remembered, had always been concerned about his public image. Just how concerned, I would soon know.

"It was just after six o'clock that evening when I telephoned his flat. I thought he might well be home from the studio by then. The bell rang half a dozen times. Then he answered. I was over the first hurdle.

"I said, 'Max, this is Walter Haines.' I won't pretend I wasn't nervous. My voice was shaky, my heart was pounding, and I could hardly hold the receiver in my slippery hand. But the nervousness was just right for the planned scenario.

" 'Good God!' he exclaimed. 'What the hell do you want?'

"I said, 'I need your help, Max. I need it terribly. Laura's here. I don't know why she came to *me*, but she did. She's in a frightful state. She says she's still in love with you in spite of everything. She says she can't live without you. I've tried to calm her but I can't. She says she's got to see you. She wants a—a reconciliation.'

" 'Not a hope,' Ryland said. 'Give her a sedative.'

" 'Max, listen. She's desperate. She's threatening to kill herself, and I think she will. She's locked herself in a bedroom and the window's open. She says she'll throw herself out if you don't come. Max, you could pretend—say you're sorry, say *anything*—just to quieten her down. Just to tide things over. I'm thinking of her—of her life. There's a concrete terrace under the window. I'm begging for her life. You could soothe her . . . Max, I'm scared. . . .'

" 'You always were,' Ryland said. 'I'm not getting mixed up in this. It's no affair of mine.'

" 'It will be if there's an inquest,' I said. 'Then everything will come out. How you treated her, how you planned a sex party at your flat, how you abused her and struck her and threw her out because she wouldn't play. What do you think the coroner will say? How long do you think you'll be a TV hero after that . . . ? God, now she's screaming at me. I think she's going to jump . . . I'll have to call the police. . . .'

"There was a pregnant silence—for a couple of seconds, perhaps. Then Ryland said, 'Okay, tell her I'll come. Tell her I'm on my way. I'll be with you in half an hour.'

" 'Thanks, Max,' I said. 'Please hurry. . . .'

"I hung up, dripping with sweat. It had worked. It had worked because he thought I was a pathetic little man, who couldn't harm him, who wouldn't dream of lying to him. I drew on my gloves. I went out to the garage and collected the knife and the cudgel. I tucked the knife under a corner of the groundsheet on the lawn. I struggled into my overalls in the kitchen, zipping them up to my chin and pulling the sleeves well down. Then I stationed myself by the open rear door of the garage, just outside it on the paved strip that separated it from the lawn and a little to the right of it as I faced the road, so that I wouldn't be seen. I had the cudgel ready. And I waited. Dusk was just beginning to fall.

"I was terribly scared. If this narrative sounds matter-of-fact to you, Superintendent, it's only because everything's over now. At the time I was shaking like a leaf. It seemed hours before he came—though it couldn't have been much more than twenty minutes. His Jaguar turned into the driveway, lights blazing. I'd left the garage doors open at the front, too, and he came on till the car was right inside. The engine died and the lights went off. I heard the car door slam. I called out to him, 'I'm here, Max—at the back. Under the window. Come on through.'

"He walked through the garage, unsuspecting. As he

emerged, he was looking away from me, toward the window of the bedroom where I'd left a light on. I brought the cudgel down with all my strength on the back of his head. I had absolutely no qualms about taking him unawares. This wasn't a sporting event. And don't think it didn't need courage. I was taking my life in my hands. I'd lived through this moment a hundred times, and I knew the risks. I knew I had only one chance, only one blow. And it had to be good, or I was finished.

"It *was* good—even though the club snapped in my hand at the impact. Ryland pitched forward on to the grass and lay prone, face down. No sound came from him. I heaved him over on to his back and dragged him on to the floorboard stretcher. Then I took the knife from under the groundsheet and stabbed him. He twitched slightly at the first blow, but after that he was still. I stabbed him many times, wildly, savagely, each blow a symbol of my hate and a settlement of my account. I struck hard to the boards, as I'd planned, so that there'd be no question about where he'd been killed. The execution took, perhaps, twenty seconds. After the fifth or sixth blow I stopped, because he was unmistakably dead. And so, finally, was my fear of him.

"I got up from my knees and walked, a little shakily, through the garage and closed the front doors behind the Jaguar. Now I had absolute privacy. I wheeled out the boat trolley, and got one end of the stretcher on to it, and heaved until the load was balanced. I arranged my two stout planks so that they provided a run-up from the ground to the back of the station wagon. Then I hauled the whole thing up—stretcher and body and trolley—into the car. I put the two pieces of the broken club and the run-up boards in as well. The knife was firmly in the corpse, transfixing it. I bundled up the groundsheet from the corners, to prevent any blood leaking out if there was any, took off my overalls, and put these two things also in the car, with my rubber gloves. Then I closed and locked the car doors, and locked up the garage, front and back.

"I took my shoes off in the kitchen and inspected them. There was no blood on them, and I put them back on. I went quickly up to the bathroom to look myself over. Hair, face, neck, hands. . . . The only blood I could see was on my right wrist—a little had worked its way between the overall sleeve and the top of the rubber glove—and I washed it off. The time was just seven o'clock, and I was almost ready to leave. I rang Reliable Motors for a minicab, locked the back door of the house and fastened the windows, switched off all but the front outside light, and waited in the hall with my luggage. The cab arrived, as you know, just before seven thirty. I caught the plane at Heathrow and flew to Lisbon.

"I felt not a twinge of regret or remorse—only a very satisfying sense of achievement. I no longer had to despise myself—I had carried out my plan with courage. It had been a good plan—and so far it had worked without a hitch. Naturally I had moments of anxiety in Portugal. Anxiety lest the hole in the chalet floor should be discovered (though with Ryland dead, that was less likely than ever); anxiety lest someone familiar with the place should notice that the boat trolley was missing; anxiety lest for some unforeseeable reason the garage at Green Boughs should be entered, and its macabre contents discovered. But since no one had a key to the garage except myself and since, short of a burglary, no one would have any cause to break in, that also seemed most unlikely. I was not, in fact, seriously troubled by these hypothetical and improbable dangers, and I managed to get quite a lot of enjoyment from my trip.

"I flew back to London, as you know, on Friday, October eighteenth—eager to finish the job and put the whole Ryland episode behind me. The house and garage were exactly as I'd left them, except that the body was getting a bit high. Another week or two, and perhaps someone *might* have broken in!

"I started at once to put my residual plans into effect. The first thing was to get rid of Ryland's Jaguar. Late that night—or I should say in the early hours of the morning—I drove the car down to the chalet and put it in his garage. Once again, the place was completely deserted, and the chalet showed no sign of having been entered. The dinghy was where I'd left it, and the pile of wood looked undisturbed. Nothing untoward had occurred—and there were no problems. But, without a car, I had to make a small physical effort to get back. In the hour or so before daybreak, I walked the three miles to Springford bus station. On the way I took the opportunity to pop into a phone box and look up the number of the local police, which I knew I should need later. I returned to town by an early train from Colchester.

"I was now all set for the final operation, which was bound to be a grueling one. I spent a quiet day, catching up on my sleep, and making sure I had overlooked nothing of importance. Late that night I put my bag of tools into the station wagon and drove it and all its contents to the chalet. There was a hint of moon—just enough to help me.

"I went quickly to work—wearing my overalls and gloves, and once more in stockinged feet. Using my two stout planks again, I successfully lowered the trolley and its gruesome burden to the ground. I opened up the chalet, and laid the planks down between the door and the hole in the floor to take the trolley wheels—which otherwise might have left suggestive tracks. Then I wheeled in the corpse on its stretcher. I had a little problem with the battens I'd fixed to the underside, but by raising each end of the stretcher in turn, I finally managed to unscrew and free them without taking the whole thing apart. The floorboards slotted neatly into place with a bit of maneuvering, and I screwed them down as carefully as I'd taken them up. By the time I'd finished, no one would have guessed that they'd ever been disturbed. This, clearly, was the place where Ryland had been killed. I put the chalet key in the corpse's pocket, wiped the knife handle that protruded from its chest, put the trolley back under the outboard dinghy, put the two planks and the two battens into the station wagon, put the broken bits of the club on the floor behind the door, picked up my tool bag and torch, took a last careful look around the room, and let myself out, pulling the door shut behind me. Then I drove the car back to town, and fell exhausted into bed.

"First thing next morning, quite recovered after several hours of sleep, I gave the interior of the station wagon a thorough cleaning, a real sousing with a hose. I didn't stop till I was quite certain that any traces of blood there might have been had been well and truly washed away.

"On that same Sunday morning I walked to a phone box near the house, dialed Springford police station, and reported that there was a body at Tamarisks. I spoke in a whisper, for obvious reasons. I made the call because I knew that the longer the body lay in the chalet undiscovered, the more difficult it might become to check back on Ryland's last known movements, and to say with reasonable accuracy when he had died. My alibi, of course, would depend on both these things.

"Once the body was found, and the main facts established, the alibi was unbreakable—as you, Superintendent, will be the first to agree. I knew I would come under suspicion; I knew I would be questioned; but I knew I would quickly be dismissed from the case—which is precisely what happened. I wouldn't have given the killing of Ryland a moment's subsequent thought if it hadn't been for your unfortunate array of circumstantial evidence against Tim Burrows. Maybe you could never have convicted him—but I couldn't take the risk. I have many weaknesses, but letting another man suffer for my actions is not one of them. The possibility that a case might be made out against someone else was the one thing, the only thing, that my plans took no account of."

XII

Maude had said almost nothing during my long narrative. His only interruptions had been to clarify some minor point, some ambiguity of wording. Mostly he had just stared at me in a fascinated way, as the recording tape moved on.

The silence after I'd finished would have pleased any actor—for it was the silence of shock, not of boredom or indifference. Whatever else I'd done, or failed to do, I had certainly held the rapt attention of the two policemen.

It was I who spoke first. "I'm pretty dry after all that, Superintendent. Do you mind if I get myself a glass of water?" Maude waved a hand in a help-yourself gesture, and I went into the kitchen and drained two glasses.

When I got back, Sergeant Wilcox was changing the tape in his machine. As I sat down he started it up again.

Maude said, "Well, Mr. Haines—that was a remarkable confession. One of the most remarkable I have ever heard."

"The truth often is remarkable," I said tritely.

"A most ingenious alibi. And a most impressive technical achievement. I'm bound to say it would never have occurred to me that the floorboards might have been removed."

"I don't think you can blame yourself for that, Superintendent. It probably wouldn't have occurred to Sherlock Holmes, either."

"But it occurred to you."

"The initiator always has the advantage. And plotting is my business."

"The risks were obviously enormous. Almost anything could have gone wrong, at any stage. But you weren't deterred."

"On the contrary, I was stimulated. The greater the hazards, the greater the triumph. I think I've made it clear that I wasn't *just* getting rid of Ryland. I was proving something—a very great deal—to myself. Self-respect isn't regained by a walkover victory."

"You regard it as your finest hour, eh?"

"To be honest, I think I do."

"H'm . . . Of course, Mr. Haines, you realize that any confession needs to be confirmed—or disproved—by some independent evidence before it can be finally accepted or rejected."

"I do realize that," I said. "I'll give you all the help I can."

"Good. . . . Have you a phone extension here?"

"Yes, there's one in the study."

"May I use it?"

"By all means. You'll find the study at the end of the hall—the last room on the left."

Maude went off, closing the sitting-room door behind him. After a moment I heard the study door being shut, too. He was taking good care I didn't catch any of the conversation. I wondered what he was up to. I lit a cigarette—a rare thing for me. Sergeant Wilcox still hadn't opened his mouth, and I wasn't sure he could. His gaze was averted, as though he found the situation embarrassing. I smoked the cigarette in silence, down to the stub. Then Maude came back. There was nothing to be read in his face. He stood looking at me, thoughtfully. He didn't seem at all hostile—he was kind of speculatively neutral.

"One thing that surprises me," he said, "is all this handyman activity of yours. I wouldn't have thought of you as being particularly good with tools."

"Well, you're wrong there," I told him. "Carpentry has been a hobby of mine for years. Perhaps you'd like to see the summerhouse I built?"

"Yes," he said, "I would."

I took him down to the bottom of the garden and showed him the structure. "This is what I ordered a supply of timber for. Rather more than I needed—but it's hard to size up a job before you start."

Maude walked around the summerhouse a couple of times, examining the fastenings and the joinery. "Very good," he said. "Very good indeed. . . . Are you *sure* you built it?"

"I'd hardly say so if it wasn't true, Superintendent. You could very easily check."

"Yes. . . ." He glanced around the close-cropped

lawn. "Would you care to show me where the stretcher was lying when you stabbed Ryland?" He was being very polite.

I indicated the area, and he studied it closely. "There don't seem to be any marks," he said.

"No. . . . You may remember we'd had a long dry spell. The ground was very hard."

He bent lower. "No signs of any pressure on the grass."

"Well, there wouldn't be, would there? After all, it's nearly three weeks now since it happened. And I gave the lawn its last autumn cut this morning—as you can see. Chewed it up a bit with the mower, I'm afraid—the blades need adjusting. . . . You won't find any traces of blood, either. The stretcher was on a plastic ground-sheet, remember."

"I remember very well. What happened to the ground-sheet?"

"I got rid of it. I thought at first it would be enough if I washed the blood off in the bath, as there wasn't very much of it, but then I noticed a small crack that I wasn't too sure I could get clean. So I screwed it up into a bundle again and burned it in the incinerator. It wasn't difficult. You know how plastic goes in a hot fire—it kind of melts away."

"What about your overalls?"

"They went into the incinerator, too. I couldn't actually see any blood on them—they were already pretty stained with oil and paint—but I knew that one spot would be a spot too much, and I couldn't take any chances."

"Where are the two stout planks you used for the trolley?"

"I sawed them up into small pieces and burned them. The trolley wheels had left faint marks on the wood."

"And the battens you used to hold the floorboards together? I suppose you burned those, too?"

"Yes, I did."

"You certainly seem to have been playing with fire," Maude said—with grim relish of his own joke. "When exactly did this orgy of destruction take place, Mr. Haines?"

"Well, let me see. . . . It was on the Sunday afternoon, the same day that I phoned the police and reported the body. I made a clean sweep of everything."

"You went to all that trouble, knowing that you'd already given yourself an absolutely unbreakable alibi?"

"I thought it wiser. Even the best of alibis falls apart sometimes—and if mine had done so, the police might well have asked to search the premises. I felt happier when I'd got rid of all the relics. I knew then that I was safe."

"H'm. Well, let's see if there's anything left of the relics." Maude walked over to the incinerator and lifted the lid. I stood back, not troubling to look—I knew what was there. The incinerator was about half full of old ash and tiny unconsumed fragments. Maude picked out a small piece of charred wood, about the size of a thumb-nail; a tiny remnant of cloth that had once been part of my overalls, and that crumbled in his hand; and a scrap of curled and tortured plastic. He regarded the objects without pleasure—then tossed them back.

He felt the bottom of the incinerator. "It's warm," he said.

I nodded. "It would be. I burned a lot of leaves in it this morning. They pile up at this time of year, and I'm not interested in compost heaps. It was my wife who was the gardener."

Maude looked in the incinerator again, examined the ash, stirred it with a finger, and came up with a small tight knot of leaves, scorched outside, damp in the center. "Yes," he said. He replaced the lid. "What happened to your rubber gloves? Did you burn those, too?"

"No—I thought they might make rather a stink. I split them open, so that they were obviously useless, and put them with the rest of the rubbish in the trash can. Wrapped in newspaper."

"When was that?"

"Oh, on the same day—the Sunday."

"And, of course, the trash can has been emptied since then."

"Yes, naturally. It was emptied on the Monday."

"Just once a week they call, eh?"

"No, twice a week."

"When was the last call?"

"The garbage truck was here this morning, as a matter of fact. One of those noisy contraptions that chew everything to pulp on the spot."

"Very convenient," Maude said. I wasn't sure whether he was referring to the method, or the date, or both. He stood for a moment in thought. Then he tried a new tack. "If, as you say, Mr. Haines, you screwed your two battens across the ends of the floorboards to make your stretcher, the boards would presumably have additional screw holes in them now. That would give us some corroboration of your story."

I shook my head. "That's a nonstarter, I'm afraid. I used the holes that were already there—the ones made by the screws that had fastened the boards to the joists.

{ 130 }

And the same screws. . . . It would have been very amateurish to overlook an obvious point like that."

"I suppose so," Maude said. "Well, we must keep on trying . . . Perhaps now you'd show me exactly where you were standing when you struck Ryland with the club."

I took up a position at the side of the rear garage door, which was open. Maude walked the length of the garage, turned, and came back through it until he was level with me. "Which was the lighted window?" he asked. I pointed, and he turned toward it, and I gave him a gentle tap on the back of the head with my hand. "No real difficulty, you see. Anyone coming through in the dark, and not suspecting an attack, would be bound to look toward the light. That was why I stood on this side. That was what I was counting on."

Maude grunted. He seemed to be measuring with his eye the few feet to the edge of the lawn. "And Ryland fell on the grass."

"Yes. He gave a sort of sideways stagger, and then fell full-length. About here." I indicated.

"And you turned him over and dragged him on to the boards."

"As I told you."

"M'm. . . . Of course, you were taking quite a risk in those few moments, weren't you? The front garage doors were open. The garden was illuminated to some extent by the lighted window. If anyone had been passing the house at the time, he could have seen right through. He might even have seen you strike Ryland."

"That's true," I said. "I realized it was possible. But there were two cars in the garage, partly obstructing the view—and the odds against anyone passing and looking in during those few crucial seconds were high. This isn't a busy neighborhood. Anyway, it was a chance I had to take. I had no choice. All I could do was shut the front doors as soon as possible afterward—which I did."

Maude seemed satisfied with my reply. "Right. . . . Now here's another question. How would you say Ryland was lying on the stretcher, after you'd dispatched him? I'm talking about his position. Was he lying more or less parallel with the boards, or was he perhaps at an angle?"

I considered. "Well—I didn't notice at the time, of course, I was far too concerned with other things—but now you mention it, I do have a mental picture of the body on the boards after I took it to the chalet—and I'd say it was pinned at a slight diagonal."

"It was, eh?"

"Am I wrong about that? It was only an impression."

"No—as a matter of fact you're not wrong. . . . Tell me more, now, about the actual stabbing. Was it easy? Difficult? Any particular problems?"

"All I can remember," I said, "is that I had a little trouble getting the knife out once or twice. I suppose that was when it pierced the boards—or maybe when it struck bone. I wouldn't know. I was hardly in a state to be making mental notes!"

"Fair enough. . . ." Maude turned and gazed out over the woodland view, and then to right and left. I guessed he was trying to estimate how far away the nearest houses were—there were rooftops just visible through the trees—and whether there was any chance that sounds might have been heard. I knew it was most unlikely, and I imagine he thought the same. Anyhow he didn't say anything.

Instead he went back into the garage. He examined my

rack of well-kept tools, and my tool bag, and asked me which screwdriver I had used on the boards, and I pointed it out. Then he turned his attention to the station wagon. "Is it unlocked?" he asked.

"Yes."

He opened all the doors, and gave the interior a thorough inspection. The car was hardly in showroom condition, but it was pretty clean. He examined the floor, the seats, the sides. "You said you hosed it, Mr. Haines. When exactly was that?"

"On that same Sunday morning," I told him. "After I got back from depositing the corpse."

He ran his finger over the inside of the rear window. "Dust," he said.

"It's nearly three weeks ago," I reminded him. "I did a very thorough job at the time. I'm afraid you won't find any traces of blood."

"I'm sure I shan't." Maude closed the doors. "Well, there it is. No independent evidence so far. One way and another, you seem to have covered *all* your tracks."

"Yes," I said. "I'm sorry. At the time, of course, it was what most concerned me—not to leave a single clue. It never occurred to me that I'd be forced into a confession, and that evidence would be needed to support it. I see your difficulty, and I wish I could help. . . ." Then an idea struck me. "I suppose there might be a bit of *negative* evidence at the chalet. I'm thinking of the floorboards. I know they were very tightly fitted together, but if Ryland had been stabbed in the chalet—he wasn't, but if he had been—a little blood *might* have seeped down to the concrete, or whatever the foundations are made of, underneath the boards. The lack of it would tend to bear out what I've said."

"And the presence of it would do the opposite, Mr.

Haines, wouldn't it? As a matter of fact, my men are looking into that right now."

"Really? You're a fast thinker, Superintendent. I suppose that's what you were telephoning about. . . . Of course, there might have been another bit of evidence, something more positive, if we'd thought of it in time. I told you I was very careful with those screws—but I dare say the brass heads might have shown a minute scratch or two—maybe under a microscope. Some slight suggestion of disturbance. . . . However, if your men have taken the boards up, there'll be scratches anyway."

Maude said, rather shortly, "You can't look under floorboards without taking them up, can you? I had to make a choice." I could understand his annoyance. He stumped off toward the house, and I followed him.

As we reentered the sitting room, Sergeant Wilcox rose and cleared his throat, as though inviting attention. I thought he was going to say "Permission to speak, sir?" but he didn't have to. Maude said, "What is it, Sergeant? Something on your mind?"

"It was just a thought, sir. Maybe you've asked the question yourself. I was wondering why Mr. Haines bothered to wipe the knife handle if he was wearing gloves all the time."

Wilcox wasn't so dumb, after all.

Maude looked at me, black eyebrows raised. "Well, Mr. Haines?"

I said, "That's an easy one, Superintendent. I'm a pessimist. A belt-and-braces man, as my wife used to say. I was pretty sure I *had* always worn gloves, but I'd handled the knife so much and in such a variety of circumstances—some of them rather upsetting—that there was always the chance I might have slipped up and inadvertently touched it with a bare hand. And of course a single print would have been the end of me. . . . I wiped the knife handle as a final precaution—that's all. . . ."

As I finished my explanation, the telephone rang. I picked up the receiver, listened . . . then handed it to Maude. "It's for you, Superintendent."

"I'll take it in the study," Maude said.

XIII

He was away much longer this time. I waited patiently. Where police activities are concerned, you haven't much choice. It must have been well over half an hour before he reappeared. By then I had smoked three cigarettes. There was a look of quiet satisfaction on his face as he rejoined us.

I said, "Well—did they find any blood under the boards?"

"No, Mr. Haines, they didn't. As you told me, the boards were laid very close together. Nothing could have got through. . . . However, there has been an interesting development."

I waited.

"When I telephoned before, I told my men to let young Burrows off the hook. I could hardly hold him when someone else had confessed to the crime."

"Of course not," I said. "I'm glad his troubles with the police are over."

"My men explained to him that you had confessed to the murder."

"Well," I said, "I doubt if he'll blame me for killing Ryland. Our views about the man must have been very similar."

"He didn't blame you at all, Mr. Haines. He merely said that he'd never heard such a load of rubbish in all his life. He was referring to your account of what happened."

"He's hardly in a position to judge," I said.

"He thinks he is. You see, he also confessed to the murder. He said he'd been wanting to for some time, and this clinched it. He said he wasn't going to have anyone else take the blame for what he'd done. Exactly as you did. Suddenly, it seems, the world is full of altruists . . . ! So he came clean and told the whole story."

"You mean," I said, "that he told *his* story."

"If you prefer it that way."

"I certainly do. What *was* his story? May I know?"

"I'll give you the gist of it, certainly." Maude produced a notebook. Its pages were covered with shorthand writing. The Superintendent had risen high in his profession, but he could still do the basic stuff when the need arose.

"The story," he said, "unlike yours, is a very simple one. It begins with Kathie—with Burrows' feelings for her, and his anger over her seduction. As we supposed, he *did* go to the chalet and confront Ryland—even though he knew he was no match for the man physically. Ryland told him to go to hell. Burrows hit him, and they had a short scrap in which Burrows took practically all the punishment. Ryland threw him out, and Burrows went off to nurse his injuries and his anger—and his misery at having lost Kathie. That was in early July. . . ."

Maude paused, looking ahead through his notes. "Now we move right on to October fourth. Burrows says that at about nine o'clock that evening, he took a stroll along the seawall in the direction of the chalet, as he often did. As far as he knew, he was quite alone. It was a mild night, with a glimpse of moon. As he drew near to the chalet, he saw that there was a light in the sitting room, and that the door was open. He stood still, and watched. Presently Ryland came out, stayed for a moment silhouetted in the doorway, and then climbed the seawall and moved off at a leisurely pace in the opposite direction, away from Burrows, gazing out over the creek. Burrows guessed that he'd only just arrived, and had gone off to check that his boat was OK—nothing more, since he'd left the chalet door open behind him. A quick look, understandable to any yachtsman. . . . This was the first time Burrows had seen Ryland since their one-sided scrap and at the sight of him, all the old fury came surging back. He says he didn't think of consequences—not at the time. All he could think of was what Ryland had done to him. He dropped down to the garage and picked up a chunk of wood from the pile. He pulled off his clumping seaboots and slipped into the chalet in his stockinged feet and waited behind the door. In a few minutes he heard returning footsteps. As Ryland stepped through the door, Burrows struck him on the back of the head. Ryland stumbled forward, fell, and rolled over on his back, unconscious. Burrows' club had broken at the impact, and he needed a better weapon to finish Ryland off. He went to the knife drawer and grabbed a knife and stabbed Ryland repeatedly as he lay on the floor. He says he went on stabbing because he was afraid, even then, that Ryland might still have the strength to rise up and grapple with him."

Again Maude studied his notes.

"It was only when Ryland was clearly dead that Burrows began to think of his own danger. His hatred of Ryland was well known in the district, and it seemed certain that the police would get around to him quite soon. The knife handle, with his prints on it, was obviously the most damning piece of evidence, and he wiped it clean with his handkerchief. Then he switched off the lights, pulled the door shut behind him, drew on his seaboots, and hurried back to his houseboat to clean up. The only blood he found was on the right sleeve of the gray woolen shirt he'd been wearing—but it was quite a big patch, and quite unmistakably blood. He tried to soak it out in hot water—which of course merely fixed it. So he tied the shirt to a large stone, and later that night when the creek was full, he rowed out and dumped it in the channel. As he can't say just where he dropped it, and as the water is too muddy for divers to see beyond their noses, it seems very unlikely that we shall recover it.

"That's almost the end of Burrows' story—but not quite. Two weeks passed, and the body hadn't been discovered, and there seemed no immediate reason why it should be. Burrows felt no regrets over what he'd done— rather the opposite—but the thought of Ryland lying there rotting only a few hundred yards away was more than he could stomach. So on the third Sunday morning he telephoned the local police from a box—speaking in a whisper, as someone had done in a TV thriller he'd watched, to disguise his voice. And that's his story. . . .

"*Now* what have you to say, Mr. Haines?"

XIV

I was silent for a moment or two, reflecting on the turn of events. Finally I said, "Well, if Tim Burrows told your people that, Superintendent, I'm sorry for him. That's all I can say—I'm very sorry for him."

"You sound as though you don't think his story is true."

"Of *course* it isn't true," I said in a tone of exasperation. "What have you and I been talking about for all these hours? How could it be true, when I killed Ryland myself?"

"Then why should he have said what he did? Why should he be so anxious to take the blame for something he didn't do?"

I shrugged. "That's hard to say. . . . Though I can think of a few possible explanations."

"Such as?"

"Well, it isn't only the guilty who get satisfaction from

confession, is it? A lot of people confess to crimes they haven't committed. You know that, Superintendent, as well as anyone—I'm sure I don't need to quote cases. You know how they ring up the police—'My name's so-and-so, and I killed Mr. A.' 'My name's so-and-so, and I planted the bomb at B.' You know how they walk into police stations and try to give themselves up—when they had nothing whatever to do with the crime. You must have a file on such people a mile long."

"True," Maude said. "But they're usually very stupid or unbalanced or both. I wouldn't put Burrows in either category. Would you?"

"He's certainly not stupid," I agreed. "Unbalanced is another thing. Of course, there are degrees. But if he's confessed to something he didn't do, I'd say he's in need of treatment. I'd say he's disturbed. Considering what he's been through, it's not all that surprising."

"I know he's had a bad time," Maude said. "But scarcely bad enough to send a sane man round the bend."

"That's your judgment, Superintendent. You could be wrong. . . . Aren't you perhaps underrating the effects of prolonged police interrogation on a high-strung man? On top of everything else. . . . How long have you had him at the station for questioning?"

"About thirty hours. . . . But I hope you're not suggesting, Mr. Haines, that he succumbed to third-degree methods. You should know us better than that."

"I'm not suggesting thumbscrews, Superintendent. But I do know how you chaps work when you think you've got your man but lack the evidence—especially in a murder case. The relays of officers, the endless repetition of questions, the shouting, the cajoling, the relentless pressure. I'm not criticizing you for it—I know you have to do it. All I'm saying is that it could have been too much for Tim. He was already under severe strain. Maybe he decided it was easier to give up, and tell you what you wanted to hear. He could always retract afterward. It's happened over and over again."

"Burrows has been well treated," Maude said stiffly. "He hasn't been unduly harassed. He hasn't been wakened in the night and questioned under bright lights. He hasn't been deprived of sleep. He hasn't been bullied. He hasn't been subjected to undue pressure. He's in excellent physical shape. He may have found his ordeal rather grueling—as anyone would—but his interrogation wasn't severe enough to break down an *innocent* man. . . . No, Mr. Haines—the chain of cause and effect was something quite different. What provoked Burrows to confess was learning about *your* confession. He was adamant that you had had nothing to do with it; he was determined to take all the responsibility on himself. Which I can well understand, if he killed Ryland. Fundamentally decent men, caught up in a situation that leads them to murder, often do admit the killing in the end. But— and I repeat—if he *wasn't* guilty, why would he wish to take responsibility? *Why?* I'm still waiting for a convincing explanation of that, Mr. Haines."

I'll say this for Maude. He wasn't a hustler—not in discussion. He waited patiently and courteously—indeed, almost respectfully—while I pondered the matter. And I had quite a lot to ponder.

"Well," I said at last, "I'm not a psychologist. I don't know what's been going on in Tim Burrows' mind, any more than you do. So I don't *know* the answer to your problem. All I can do is suggest a possible explanation—which is this. I think it's likely that Tim wanted to *claim* the killing of Ryland. Not at first, because he didn't need to; he was the only suspect and was probably going to be charged anyway—but after I appeared on the scene. I think that's why he ridiculed my confession—he didn't want anyone else to take the credit—or as you would say, the blame—for something he would have liked to do himself, but didn't. . . . The thing is, he's still desperately in love with Kathie—and I'm pretty sure he hasn't altogether given up hope of getting her back. But he's troubled by a sense of failure in the past. He wasn't around to protect his girl when Ryland assaulted her. He was worsted in a fight with Ryland, as everyone in the district knows—including, no doubt, Kathie herself. So, irrational though it may seem, he feels he's shown up badly in her eyes. He thinks she regards him as inadequate. He partly shares her view. Somehow he has to reinstate himself—with her, and with himself. I would guess—and it is only a guess—that he's claiming Ryland's killing as the most effective, the most dramatic way of showing Kathie there are no limits to what he'd do for her, no sacrifice he wouldn't make on her behalf. It's not beyond reason. A man will go to extraordinary lengths to restore his image in the sight of someone he loves. It could even work. . . . I may be way off beam, Superintendent—but that's my theory. That's my explanation."

"You think," Maude said, "that confessing to murder would be likely to bring a girl back to the murderer?"

"I think it's possible that a woman might return with love and gratitude to a man who had killed to avenge an outrageous assault on her. Heavens, women have been doing just that through all the centuries. . . . A man under great stress of mind could certainly *persuade* himself it was possible."

"It would be a big sacrifice for an uncertain end," Maude said. "In Burrows' case, ten years in jail at the very least, I would say."

"Oh, come, Superintendent! In these days of diminished responsibility for practically everyone? 'I blew up the pub because I'm an idealist, sir.' 'I cracked the crib because I was neglected in my childhood, sir.' 'I stole the goods because I am underprivileged, sir.' 'Very understandable! Six-months suspended sentence—and don't do it again.' "

Maude gave a half-smile. On one thing, at least, he saw eye to eye with me. But he stuck to his view on Burrows. "Ten years," he repeated. "It would have been willful murder—deliberate, calculated murder—with no *immediate* provocation. . . . Ten years, undoubtedly."

"Well," I said, "you could be right about that—but Tim might have seen his prospects differently. Don't forget that when he talked to your men, my confession was already on the record and known to him. It must be almost impossible for an innocent man to believe he can actually be sent to prison when someone else has confessed to the crime. He could think he was making a gesture without penalty."

Maude said, "H'm," and sat frowning. He was clearly considering all that I had said—and considering it carefully. His final headshake was less than emphatic. "Well, your theory is interesting, Mr. Haines. It could even turn out to be true. At the moment, however, it doesn't convince me."

"Then you'll have to supply your own explanation,

Superintendent. . . . The one certain fact is that I killed Ryland, and Tim didn't."

At that point our inconclusive discussion ended. There was the sound of a powerful car turning into the drive. Almost immediately there was a ring at the bell.

"That will be for us," Maude said. "Come along, Mr. Haines."

So this was it! Maude was going to take me in, in spite of his doubts. I braced myself for the police cell I had so often written about.

"I shall need a few things, shan't I?" I said.

"Only your driving licence, sir! I've had Ryland's Jaguar brought over. A fine car. Very responsive. Very different from your station wagon—or even your wife's Rover. You told me you drove the Jaguar from here to the chalet at night. Right—let's go for a drive, and see how you get on."

I followed him out to the garage. By now darkness had fallen. A uniformed figure stepped from the shadows and saluted Maude. I walked around to the driver's seat. The car's sidelights were on. So was the interior light. I slid in behind the wheel. Maude settled himself beside me. I turned the ignition key, and the panel lit up. I looked for the light switches and found them. I switched off the interior light and switched on the headlights—fumbling a bit over dipping them. I started the engine and backed the car out of the garage.

"You mustn't expect perfection," I told Maude. "This is only the third time I've handled her, remember."

"The *third* time?" he said.

"That's right. The first time was back in May, when Ryland thought I'd enjoy driving home from the creek. The second time was when I took it to the chalet, the night before the final placing of the body. This is the third time."

Maude grunted.

"Where do you want me to go?" I asked.

"Anywhere you like. Just keep moving."

I drove to the end of the road, and turned left. I felt quite at ease behind the wheel. If you've driven a car, however infrequently, it doesn't take long to get used to it again. We drifted around the suburban roads for a few minutes, then turned into a main one with three lanes each way. I opened the throttle, and we shot past two buses and a lorry in about one second flat. It was a most exhilarating feeling.

I said, "I believe this car will do about a hundred and thirty, Superintendent, but we are in a built-up area. How fast would you like me to go?"

Maude said in a surly tone, "Okay, you've passed your test. Back to the house."

He made no further comment on my performance with the Jaguar. He made no further comment on anything until we were once more in the sitting room. He seemed to be turning something over in his mind—some new ploy, I guessed. And I was right. It was to do with time-and-motion.

"As I understand it, Mr. Haines," he said, "you drove to Springford on three separate nights in October."

I thought about it. "That's right," I said.

"Well, now, I'd like you to give me a rough idea of the timing of each journey. When you set out—and when you returned."

"By all means. The first occasion was—let me think—October second. That was the night of my reconnaissance. I left here in the station wagon around midnight, reached Springford at about two in the morning, and got back here around five."

Maude nodded. He wasn't taking notes. Sergeant Wilcox had turned the tape recorder on again.

"And on the fourth, you inveigled Ryland here, and killed him?"

"Yes."

"Then, on the night of the eighteenth, after your return from Portugal, you drove the Jaguar down to the chalet and left it in the garage. How about the timing of that journey?"

"I set out from here about four in the morning, arrived at the chalet around six, parked the Jaguar, walked to Springford, and caught a train from Colchester. I can't remember the exact time of the train—it was somewhere around nine o'clock. I was back in the house some time before eleven."

"And on Saturday the nineteenth, you drove the station wagon to the chalet, with the body and all your gear in it, and finished the job."

"Yes. I left here about eleven at night, arrived at Springford about one, and was back I suppose around four."

"M'm. Three pretty arduous journeys, eh? Not to mention your exertions at the chalet. And during some of this period you were also very busy at home. Making your preparations, killing Ryland and getting his body into the station wagon, cleaning up afterward?"

"Yes."

"Altogether, wouldn't you say, a fairly mammoth undertaking?"

"It was—but the result was worth the effort."

"H'm. . . . Well, I'm sorry to tell you, Mr. Haines,

that the effort isn't over. I propose to reconstruct this murder of yours. In detail, from the beginning to the end. Of course, I can't compel you to take part—but I trust you will. I'd like you to hold yourself at my disposal for the next four nights and days. Starting at midnight tomorrow."

I jibbed a bit—knowing what it would involve. "It will be a complete waste of your time, Superintendent. It will only confirm what I've already told you."

"That remains to be seen."

I shrugged. "Well—if you insist. . . ." I could hardly refuse.

"In the meantime, perhaps you'd let me have your passport back."

"What, *again* . . . ? What do you think I'm going to do—flee the country? After making a voluntary confession!"

"No, I don't," Maude said. "Any more than you expected your alibi to break down—or the knife handle to have your fingerprints on it. But *you* took extra precautions. That's exactly what I'm doing. . . . I'll see you here tomorrow night, Mr. Haines—on the stroke of twelve."

XV

~~~

I took things very quietly the next day, husbanding my physical resources against the strenuous time ahead and preparing myself mentally for the repeat performance. I had a light lunch, did a bit of shopping, topped up the station wagon's gas tank, dined sensibly at a local restaurant, and in the late evening managed to catch a little sleep. It didn't exactly knit up the ravell'd sleeve of care, but it did refresh me somewhat.

Maude and Sergeant Wilcox arrived punctually at twelve. They brought with them a new pair of rubber gloves and fresh batteries for my torch. They needn't have bothered, because these items had been on my own shopping list. I wasn't in favour of Maude's charade, but I could see it was to my benefit—if establishing a confession of guilt *is* a benefit—to give him maximum cooperation at every stage.

Maude checked a few things—whether I was wearing

the same clothes and shoes as before, whether my new rubber gloves were the same size, whether I'd put the bag of tools in the station wagon. Then he ran through the night's program with me. "We're regarding today as Wednesday, October second," he said. "We're going to repeat your reconnaissance visit to the chalet. I want you to do exactly what you did then—no more, no less. Consider the sergeant and myself as spectators only. I've had a transcript made of your confession, and I shall be checking your movements all along the line. . . . Right—let's get started."

The drive to Springford was uneventful. We were now almost into November and the night was raw, but the station wagon had a good heater and there was no discomfort. We had very little conversation on the way. Whenever I began to speak, I heard the click of Wilcox's battery recorder coming into operation behind me, which was disconcerting and unconducive to chat. Besides, I had a great deal to think about.

We arrived just after two o'clock—right on schedule. The track, the seawall, and the area around the chalet looked as though they had been abandoned by the human race for several centuries. There was no moon, but the darkness was less than intense. Colchester was only nine miles away, and there was a faint reflected glow from the lighted sky above the city. I parked the car among the tamarisks, and with the policemen close behind me, went straight to work. I took the tool bag into the porch, slipped off my shoes, drew on the rubber gloves, and groped under the seat for the key. Rather to my surprise, it was on its hook. I assumed that Maude had had it put there. I opened up the chalet; the two men followed me in; and I shut the door behind them. I went through the motions of checking the curtains, and switched on my torch. Maude had his own torch, so we weren't short of light. I bent down and carefully examined the floorboards near the door. Those that had been removed and put back showed some small discolored patches, presumably where Ryland's blood had seeped out onto them. There were also two or three marks in the wood where the knife point had penetrated. Naturally I hadn't seen the boards in that condition before. I brought my torch close, and pretended to be studying the fastenings. I got up with an appropriate grunt of satisfaction, and stood back, eyeing the boards as though I was deciding which ones to take up. Then I picked out a screwdriver of the right size—the one I had shown to the Superintendent in the garage at Green Boughs—and balanced the torch on the tool bag so that it shone down. I had a little difficulty over that—it kept falling off—but I managed to fix it in the end. I blew on my gloved hands. "It's a lot colder tonight than it was the first time," I said. "I'm bound to fumble a bit." Maude nodded. "We'll make allowance, Mr. Haines." Actually I wasn't cold at all. I was sweating.

The screws came out quite easily. I knew that scratches on the heads were of no importance any more, since the police had had the boards up, but with Maude's eyes on me I still took care that the screwdriver didn't slip. He wanted an exact reproduction, and I would do my best to supply it. The job took just under half an hour. By the end of it I was not merely sweating; I was soaked. I wrapped the screws in a handkerchief and put them in the pocket of my jacket, which I'd hung on a wall hook. I prised up the loose boards, and stood them in the right order against the wall near the door. Then I picked up the torch and went over to the knife drawer. From the watchful policemen behind me, there was now not a sound. I opened the drawer and shone the torch in. The kitchen knives were kept in a separate compartment. There were half a dozen of them, of varying lengths and shapes. Two of them had long, strong blades with sharp points. Both had wooden handles of rectangular section, with sloping, flattened tops. They weren't identical, but they were nearly so. I picked one out. Maude said, "Let me see it, Mr. Haines." I gave it to him and he examined it closely. Then he gave a reluctant nod. "A fifty-percent chance, eh?" I said, "Not at all, Superintendent. . . . When you've killed a man with a knife, you don't forget what the knife looked like." It was a rather silly remark, because I should think you easily might—but Maude didn't argue. I mopped my face and neck with my shirt sleeve, and took the knife back from him and put it in the tool bag.

There was nothing more to be done inside the chalet. I opened the door, looked cautiously out, and then carried the floorboards one by one to the station wagon, the ground cold and rough under my stockinged feet. The boards weren't particularly heavy, but I had a little difficulty getting them through the tamarisk bushes in the semidarkness. Maude watched the operation from the door; Wilcox stood by the car, observing the stowage. Having neatly arranged the boards in their order, I collected my jacket and the tool bag from the chalet, closed the door, put the key in my jacket pocket, picked up my shoes, and went round to the side of the garage. By the dim light of my torch I choose a piece of wood from the pile, swung it in the air to test it, and put it in the tool bag. Then I heaved the outboard dinghy off its trailer—no problem there—and carried the trailer to the station wagon and stowed it carefully, tying it up with a piece of string to one of the seat-belt hooks. Finally I retrieved my shoes and put them on.

I felt pretty satisfied with the night's work. "The only difference from last time," I told Maude as I took the wheel again, "is that with three of us in the car and all the gear, we're going to be a bit cramped. . . . Also, that I've got cold feet."

"I'm not surprised," Maude said. "Your worst troubles are still ahead!"

The superintendent enjoyed his sardonic little jokes.

We got back to Green Boughs at five thirty in the morning, only a little behind schedule. The policemen went off in their car, and with the help of a stiff tot of whisky I managed to get an hour or two of much-needed sleep. It was a short respite. Around ten o'clock Maude returned to the house to watch my preparations for the next stage of my murder plan. He was particularly interested in the construction of the stretcher, and in certain difficulties I had with it. Even allowing for my having done it before, it wasn't all that simple to screw battens across the ends of four boards and finish up with not the tiniest gap between them. It was, in fact, an extremely delicate job—made no easier by the hampering effect of gloves. I also pointed out to Maude that on the first occasion I hadn't had a policeman breathing down my neck all the time—which he seemed to agree was relevant. Anyway I made a satisfactory job of it in the end. I put the stretcher in the garage, with the trolley, the knife, and the cudgel, and covered them with the balloon cloth—and, for the moment, that was it. By now it was almost lunchtime, and I offered Maude a drink before he left—but this time he declined. He said he'd be dropping in next day to watch my final preparations, and that he'd bring new overalls, a plastic groundsheet, and a few other props with him. I thanked him for being so helpful!

The following day, according to the game we were playing—or the duel we were fighting—was supposed to be October fourth. D day for the murder. Maude and his sergeant showed up around eleven in the morning. They had brought, in addition to the things Maude had mentioned, a bulky, six-foot dummy, which they carried through the garage to the rear garden. The reconstruction was getting more macabre by the hour—and I was liking it less and less. They watched while I spread out the new groundsheet on the lawn, and humped the stretcher from the garage, and placed it in position on the groundsheet. They watched as I collected and concealed the knife. They watched while I picked out two stout eight-foot planks from my residual store of timber. They watched while I backed the station wagon into the garage and opened its rear doors for the prospective victim. They watched as I packed my bag for a journey to Portugal that I had already undertaken. They watched every movement I made, checking at intervals with the transcript. It was hard on the nerves.

They left me alone for an hour or two in the afternoon—but at six o'clock they were back to witness the kill. Maude said he didn't require any reenactment of my telephone conversation with Ryland, or of the events immediately following Ryland's arrival—the slamming of the car door, my call to him, the walk through the garage, the blow on the head, for which the new club was lying handy. He said we'd already been over that. He suggested we should start with the dummy lying on the grass where Ryland had fallen unconscious, and the sergeant helped him move it to the spot that I indicated.

I put on my new overalls and my rubber gloves. I went upstairs and switched on the bedroom light, which shed enough of a glow over the garden to make the subsequent action possible. Maude said, "Right, Mr. Haines, carry on. Before Ryland comes round!" In all the circumstances, I thought his jocularity most misplaced. It was all very well for him! I leaned over the face-down dummy and tried to turn it over. It was extremely heavy—a good fourteen stone, I judged. It was a cloth dummy, stuffed with rustling straw, but somebody had put a lot of ballast inside as well. That was fair enough—I had no grounds for complaint. I said, "This was when I had trouble with the *real* Ryland." I heaved at the dummy, putting out all the strength I had, and finally managed to get it on to its side, and turn it over. Dragging it on to the stretcher was less difficult. The grass was smooth, and with my hands under the dummy's arms from the back, I was able to move it on to the boards in a series of heaving jerks. As soon as I'd got it in position, I grabbed the knife from under the groundsheet and made half a dozen wild stabs at its chest. There was no rib cage, this time, to get in the way, but each time the knife went through to the boards I had to work hard to pull it out again. However, I managed. My last blow was the strongest, and it left the dummy pinned to the stretcher.

I got up from my knees, boiling hot and badly out of breath.

"Very good," Maude commented. "Very efficient. I

think we can assume life is extinct! Not let's see you get into the station wagon, Mr. Haines."

"Haven't I earned a rest?" I said.

"You'd hardly have rested with a dead man on your lawn! Carry on, please."

I went through the garage and closed the front doors. I collected the trolley and put it down near the stretcher. I raised one end of the stretcher—the lighter end, where the dummy's feet were—and pulled it up onto the trolley till it was in balance, as I'd seen Ryland do with his dinghy. I paused for a moment—then, with a final heave, I got it fully on. I went back to the trolley and wheeled it to the garage. I adjusted the planks a little, to bring them in alignment with the wheels. The plan was to pull the trolley up backward. I climbed into the station wagon and grasped the trolley's long handle. "I was afraid the stretcher and its heavy load might start to slide down. If it did, I was going to tie it in some way." I hauled the trolley—and got it up the slope without too much difficulty. "But it didn't," I added. "The angle wasn't steep enough for the stretcher to move—and of course the body was pinned."

Maude was staring at me in the half-light. He didn't look jocular any more. He looked serious. Obviously he hadn't believed I could do it. Now he knew!

I went quickly through the remaining chores. I bundled up the groundsheet from the corners, and collected the unused club, and put them in the station wagon. I took off my overalls and gloves, and threw them in, too. Then I closed and locked the car doors, and locked up the garage, front and back. "Now I have to go and wash," I said. "I found blood on my wrist—remember?"

"I remember." Maude sounded rather weary—though *he'd* done nothing but stand and look. "Okay, Mr.

Haines, that's all for today. And you'll have all day free tomorrow. But tomorrow night you'll be taking the Jaguar to Springford. We'll join you here in the early hours, with the car."

I protested. "That's not fair, Superintendent. That's not a reconstruction. . . . I had a two-week break in Portugal before I took the Jaguar down."

"I'm sorry," Maude said. "We can't wait two weeks. As far as I'm concerned, tomorrow is October eighteenth."

I had a rest of sorts during the thirty hours that followed. I was free from Maude's incessant scrutiny, which was some relief. I hadn't to lug any more heavy objects around for a while. But my whole body ached from the overexertion I'd already inflicted on it, and my thoughts were too active to permit sound sleep. I dreamed, rather bloodily and horribly, which wasn't surprising. So I was still in pretty poor shape when the Superintendent and Sergeant reappeared at the ungodly hour of four o'clock in the morning and we set off once more for Springford.

I didn't attempt to conceal from Maude that I was fed to the teeth with my constantly repeated journeys to the chalet—but at least the Jaguar was fast and smooth-riding, a welcome change from the station wagon. At that time in the morning there was almost no traffic, and it was still short of six o'clock when I pulled up outside the garage at Tamarisks and cut the engine.

I sagged back in my seat. The drive had done nothing for my aches. "Well—that's that," I said.

Maude looked at me expectantly.

"Anything wrong?" I asked.

"That depends. . . . When the local police arrived on the scene, after the body was reported, the Jaguar was in the garage, and the garage was locked."

"Quite right," I said. "I drove the car in, and then locked up."

"With what?"

"With Ryland's key, of course. He had a bunch of keys in his pocket when I killed him. I'd seen him use one of them to open the garage when we were down here. I borrowed them from the corpse—and put them back in its pocket when I returned to the house. . . . Satisfied?"

"Okay," Maude said. He produced the bunch of keys. "Go ahead—open up."

I opened up, and drove the car into the garage, and locked it, and gave the keys back to Maude.

There was nothing now to hang about for, so we went off at once for Springford bus station. It was not yet daylight, but I was familiar with the route and had no trouble in conducting our plodding little party. On the outskirts of the village I stopped by a lighted telephone box. "This is where I looked up the number of the local police," I said. Maude glanced inside, saw there was a directory, and nodded—and we continued on our way. We reached the bus station after seven o'clock—and by then daylight was near.

Maude walked over to the big bus garage, which was firmly closed, and shone his torch on a wall timetable. He studied it for half a minute or so. Then he swung round on me.

"I thought you said you caught a train from Colchester around nine o'clock."

"I did."

"And you said you caught a bus into Colchester. The

first bus from here on Saturdays leaves at nine fifteen. And it was Saturday when you dumped the Jaguar."

I gave a tired sigh. "Forgive me, Superintendent, but I said nothing about catching a bus to Colchester. You can check from the record. All I said was that I walked to the bus station."

Maude consulted his transcript. It took him a little time. "That's right," he conceded—rather ungraciously, I thought. "So what happened?"

"I discovered there was no bus."

"Then why did you bring us here today?"

"I thought you wanted an exact reconstruction."

Maude gave me a dirty look. We were all getting a bit short-tempered by now. "Well—what did you do?"

"I started to walk toward Colchester. I was tired—just as I'm tired today, and for the same reasons—but I knew it was only about six miles, and anyway it seemed better to set off than to sit around here for two hours. As it happened, my luck was in. After I'd been walking for half an hour or thereabouts, I managed to thumb a lift from a car going my way, a Ford Escort. The driver was a young man with long hair—a bit wild-looking, but quite amiable. He said he was self-employed—in the building trade. He dropped me in the center of the city, and I walked to the station. . . . Maybe you'll be able to trace him."

"And maybe we won't," Maude said. "Sergeant, I think we'd better ring Colchester police station and ask them if they'll kindly send us a car."

It was almost over now, this grueling reconstruction. I was getting increasingly impatient with it. From Maude's point of view it was no doubt a sensible way of trying to disprove my confession of guilt. From my point of view it was an endurance test that would lead to nothing. I *knew* that he wouldn't be able to fault me. However, he was adamant. Another long and arduous night still lay ahead. Notionally, the night of October nineteenth. It would be one of the worst—perhaps *the* worst, as far as sheer physical effort was concerned.

I slept through much the day. I didn't need pills or whisky to put me out—it was the sleep of exhaustion. And it was much too short. I could have done with twenty hours in a row. But at eleven that night the policemen returned, and I had to drive them to Springford again in the station wagon. The three of us were squashed tightly in the front seat, because the car was loaded with gear—the stretcher, the spitted dummy, the trolley, the planks, the tool bag, the club, the gloves, the torch—everything but Uncle Tom Cobbleigh. I was already wearing the overalls, which were hot and confining and didn't make the journey any easier. . . .

It was pure hell at the chalet. I had to force myself to go through the motions, to drive my unwilling body on. Just as, I told Maude, I had had to do before. . . . Open up chalet, remove shoes, lower loaded trolley down planks, put planks on floor to take trolley wheels, wheel in dummy corpse on stretcher, maneuver stretcher off trolley, unscrew one of battens, slide that end of stretcher into available space, unscrew other batten, press whole stretcher down on joists till flush with rest of floor, line up screw holes, screw back on to joists. A good hour's work altogether—and it left me completely wrung out.

With sagging shoulders, I packed up the bits and

pieces and took them to the station wagon—the battens, the wheel-marked planks, the tool bag, the torch, the lot. I heaved the outboard dinghy back on the trolley—normally a simple operation, but now almost more than I could manage. All, of course, under the impassive gaze of the policemen. But I was through at last and was about to close up the chalet when Maude said, "Haven't you forgotten something?".

I looked around. I couldn't think what I'd forgotten. I was so deadbeat I could hardly think at all.

"You told me you wiped the knife handle, Mr. Haines."

"Of course. . . ." I took a long breath. "You do realize, don't you, Superintendent, that having a couple of coppers standing over one all the time doesn't exactly make concentration easier. And it's been pretty nerve-racking for me—all the memories—all the horror. . . . I'm not a *born* murderer, you know." I went back in, and wiped the knife handle.

As I rejoined Maude, he said, "For the sake of us all, I think I'd better take the wheel on the way back. I'm not saying you're incapable of driving—but I'm sure you wouldn't want to take the same risk twice . . . !" I barely registered his words. I slumped down in one of the rear seats—and when I woke up we were at Mill Hill Broadway, a stone's throw from the house.

XVI

I returned to the world reluctantly, but in considerably better shape after my couple of hours of sleep. My muscular aches were as bad as ever, but by the time we reached the house, I'd shaken off my mental torpor and my brain was functioning normally again.

Maude drove the station wagon into the garage and switched off the lights and the engine. "You go on in, Sergeant," he said, "we'll join you in a few minutes. Is that all right with you, sir?" I nodded, and fumbled for the house key, and gave it to Wilcox, who departed. The Superintendent clearly wanted to talk, so I moved to the front seat.

Maude turned on the interior light and gazed at me reflectively. There was a short silence. Then he said, "Well, you've given us a virtuoso performance, Mr. Haines—there's no doubt about that. A remarkable performance, a remarkable demonstration, which I can see has taxed you to the limit. Frankly I didn't think you'd have the stamina to go through with it. I'm most impressed. . . ." He paused. "However, in spite of the demonstration, I have to tell you that I don't believe a word of your story. Not a single word."

I said, "Well, that's your privilege, Superintendent. . . . But I assure you it's true."

"I don't think so. On the contrary, I think it's an invention from start to finish. I think you worked it all out, to the last detail, as though you were plotting one of your crime novels. You devised an explanation for every known fact. You took account of every hazard. You foresaw all the questions that would be asked and planned the answers that you would give. You carried through the whole operation—in your imagination. And you produced a brilliant piece of fiction."

"What an extraordinary idea," I said. "Are you serious?"

"I'm entirely serious. . . . As a fan of yours, I feel I should ask for your autograph."

"Well," I said, "I'd better sign my confession. Then you'll have it!"

"You wouldn't sound so cheerful, sir, if you thought you were going to jail."

I said, "There's no 'if' about it, Superintendent. I *know* I'm going to jail. But I faced up to that before I confessed. I shan't like it—but I shall survive. They'll probably put me in charge of the prison library. I hope so—I like quiet places. I might even be able to go on writing—which is all that is left to me anyway. After a while, they'll move me to an open prison in attractive rural surroundings. I shall be visited and cosseted by social workers, who will tell me about my 'rights.' Long before my sentence is up, I shall be released on parole. And by then my books will be selling better than ever, because of the publicity. I might even be able to push my memoirs on a Sunday newspaper. I'm not too worried."

Maude gave a faint sigh. "Mr. Haines, you've done an awful lot of talking in this case. Would you now oblige me by keeping quiet, while I give you my view of what happened?"

"By all means," I said.

"Well—I see it like this. You hated Ryland, and you wished him dead—but you're no killer. You liked Burrows—as a man, and because you had a fellow feeling for him. You'd both suffered in the same way at Ryland's hands. When I outlined the case against Burrows, you knew at once that he had killed Ryland. What's more, you believed that in the end he'd admit it. And you decided to try and save him. You were in the right frame of mind for it. With your wife gone, you had no particular purpose in life. You felt that in many ways you'd been a failure—or worse. Here, you decided, was a chance to redeem yourself. Not by murder, which you knew you'd be incapable of, but by protecting the murderer—your proxy, so to speak—at your own risk. You saw yourself as a sort of—what was the fellow's name in Dickens' book?—Sydney Carton. The man who went to the guillotine in place of someone else. 'It is a far, far better thing that I do, than I have ever done . . . ,' and all that. In your own eyes, at least, you were going to finish up a hero . . ."

I broke in there. I had to. "As I recall it," I said, "Sydney Carton made his sacrifice on behalf of someone he cared very deeply about. I don't care deeply about Tim Burrows. I like him, as I like many people, but that's all.

. . . Are you seriously suggesting that I would take the blame for a murder I hadn't done, and risk going to prison for many years, in order to save a man who was no more than an acquaintance, whom I had met only twice and spoken to only once, and who meant almost nothing to me? That really would be altruism gone mad."

"I'm not suggesting," Maude said, "that you took the blame *because* it was Burrows. The man who killed Ryland just *happened* to be Burrows. And it was the killing of Ryland that counted in your mind. I think, if the circumstances had been favorable, you would have done the same thing for *anyone* who had got rid of Ryland—as long as his motives were in line with yours. . . . Does that dispose of your objection?"

"Of the specific objection, yes—though your second suggestion seems to me just as fantastic. And of course I deny it—totally. . . . But do go on with your review, Superintendent. What, in practical terms, do you think happened? What do you think I did?"

"What happened," Maude said, "was this. You already knew a very great deal about the chalet, because of your summer visits. You'd seen how the floorboards were laid. You knew where the knives were kept. You had a clear picture of the place in your retentive mind. You got all the additional information you needed for your confession from a detailed report in the *Chronicle*—which you told me you had read—and from accounts in other newspapers. Some illustrations in the *Sketch*—showing where the body had been found, the diagonal position it was lying in, the nature and distribution of the knife thrusts, the type of knife that had been used—helped you to re-create the murder scene in your mind; and you wove the facts into your own fictional account when you learned that Burrows was in danger. . . .

"Once you'd decided to 'confess,' you destroyed everything that—merely by its negative qualities—could have disproved your story. The groundsheet that had never had any blood on it. The overalls that had been marked only by paint and oil. The gloves that had never touched anything sinister. The battens that had never had screws through them. The planks that had shown no wheel marks. . . . You cut the lawn close and churned it up with the mower, to account for the absence of any other signs. You said you had hosed this car, to explain the lack of bloodstains on it. You were very thorough—even to seeing that a few charred remnants remained in the incinerator. You had a ready explanation for the incinerator being still warm—and the ashes of burnt leaves to support your explanation—though in fact it would have been warm anyway, because you'd only that day destroyed the 'evidence.' You destroyed it, not immediately after the discovery of Ryland's body and for your own protection, as you said, but the day after I made it clear to you that Burrows was at risk—the morning of the day you called me in to hear your confession. . . . You destroyed everything; you made a clean sweep. You left me with a great big blank, a negative that I could do nothing about. It was masterly, Mr. Haines."

"It would have been if it had happened like that," I said. "But it didn't."

"It was also an obstruction of justice."

I couldn't let that pass—even though we were talking only about a theory. "You mean, surely, an obstruction of the *law?*"

"To me, the law and justice are the same thing."

"As a policeman."

"Yes."

"As a policeman, the moral questions mean nothing to you? The rights and the wrongs?"

"My duty," Maude said, "is to try to discover the truth, and then act on it. The rest is for the courts."

"How about as a man?"

"That's another matter."

"Could I put a couple of questions to you—as a man?"

"It won't get you anywhere, sir—but go ahead if you want to."

"You told me you were very happily married, Superintendent. To a young wife. But you must be very often away from home on your cases. Perhaps for quite long periods."

"Unfortunately, yes. It's a penalty of the job."

"All right. Now I'm not wishing to be in any way impertinent—I'm just putting forward a hypothesis. Suppose that a man you had previously thought of as a friend, a man supremely attractive to women, took advantage of your unavoidable absences, your preoccupation with your job, to entice your wife away from you—as Ryland did my wife. And tried to degrade her in a sexual orgy. And then struck her and threw her out, because she wouldn't go along with it. What would you do? Anything?"

"I'd probably do something," Maude said grimly.

"Of course you would. I can almost hear you thinking at this very moment, 'I'd bash the living daylights out of the sod.' Come now—be honest."

"I guess so. . . . Something like that."

"Which I'm sure, with your physique and training, you could do. But suppose this man was very powerful and muscular, and you were rather a slight man, like me—or just an average sort of man, like Tim Burrows. Then what would you do?"

Maude considered. "Frankly, I don't know."

"Would you rush to your solicitor? Would you try to take the man to court? Would you try to get monetary damages for alienation of affection?"

"That hardly seems my scene."

"How about killing him?"

Maude shrugged. "No one can tell until he's tested. . . . I know what provocation you had, Mr. Haines. I know what provocation Burrows had. I don't stand in judgment. . . . But the fact remains that you're obstructing—well, shall I say the law?"

"Do say 'the law,' Superintendent—because I believe that justice has been done, and in the only way it could have been done. The primitive way. Ryland was a destroyer. Wherever he went, he left a trail of shattered lives behind him. Not just once. Many men shatter *one* life. For him, it was a habit. And he got his deserts. The whirlwind reaped. The chickens home to roost. I'm glad I killed him—and in the same circumstances I'd do it again."

Maude said quietly, "But you *didn't* kill him, Mr. Haines."

"That's what you think. That's your view. But you can't prove it, can you? You can't point to a single weakness in my story; not the tiniest flaw, the slightest contradiction, the smallest discrepancy. And you never will be able to, because there aren't any. Truth rules out discrepancies. You can't even say that what I told you I had done was physically impossible—because you've seen for yourself that it was possible. . . . Imagine yourself, Superintendent, on the witness stand, giving evidence for the prosecution of Tim Burrows. Imagine yourself under cross-examination by the defense: 'Is it a fact, Superintendent, that a certain Walter Haines made a statement confessing to this murder?' 'Yes, it is.' 'Did you, as a result of this confession, attempt to reconstruct the murder on the lines of Mr. Haines's statement?' 'Yes, I did.' 'Did you have Mr. Haines's full cooperation in this enterprise?' 'Yes.' 'Did Mr. Haines, during the course of this reconstruction, fail to do anything that in his statement he had said he had done?' 'No.' 'So he *could* have committed the murder?' 'He *could* have, yes.' 'Thank you, Superintendent.' "

Maude was silent.

"Now take Tim Burrows," I said. "You can't prove anything about him. There's not a scrap of concrete evidence against him. Not an iota. All you've got to go on is his psychologically dubious confession—which you can't corroborate from independent sources, any more than you can corroborate mine. He and I are like the identical twins in a famous case which I'm sure you remember. You know that one of us committed the murder—but you can't prove *which* one. So whom are you going to arrest? Whom are you going to charge?"

Maude said, "That will be for the public prosecutor to decide."

"It will be a difficult decision for him, don't you think? He can hardly charge both of us with the same crime. If he charges me, Tim Burrows will undoubtedly speak out. If he decides to charge Tim, I hope he will be clear about one thing. However Tim pleads—guilty or not guilty—I shall find a way of having my say in court, and I shall swear before God, judge, and jury that every word in my confession is the exact and literal truth. Which it is. . . . Do you imagine any jury would think there was no reasonable doubt? Do you imagine you would ever get a conviction?"

Maude didn't answer. "I think I'll go and collect my sergeant," he said. "It's been a long night."

XVII

~~~

We had no more conversation of significance, and the two detectives departed in their car almost immediately. There was no suggestion that I should accompany them to headquarters, or sign the transcript of my statement, or anything official like that. There were no dark hints of further action, and no arrangements were made for a future meeting. Nothing disagreeable happened at all. The sergeant picked up his tape recorder, and Maude wished me luck with my next plot, and I presented him with an inscribed copy of a Walter Haines book that had my photograph on the dust jacket. I wrote in it, "To Superintendent Frank Maude, in memory of some interesting journeys," which seemed to tickle his fancy.

He really *did* believe I hadn't killed Ryland!

All the same, there was still a police routine to be gone through. I didn't see the Superintendent again for several days, but I sensed that his men weren't entirely inactive in the district. A police car was parked nearby during most of the next day, and two men appeared to be making inquiries at neighboring houses. I imagined they were trying to check on any loud noises or peculiar sounds coming from my direction on the evening of October fourth or after my return from Portugal—but I knew they wouldn't get anywhere. This was merely Maude going into every last detail in his usual thorough way before making his final report on the case. The inquiries must have been very discreet, for I didn't notice any of my neighbors looking askance at me as a result. I assumed that routine checks were also being made around Springford—on the Colchester road, for instance. "Do you remember seeing a man answering to this description on the morning of Saturday, October nineteenth . . .?"—with my photograph offered for inspection. "Do you know of a long-haired youth who works in the building trade and sometimes drives a Ford Escort along this road . . . ?". Or in the village itself—particularly at the houses nearest the track. "Do you remember hearing a car approaching the track in the early hours of so-and-so . . . ?" Well, I was sure nothing would come of any such activities.

My confidence seemed confirmed when, a few days later, Maude dropped in at the house and once more gave me back my passport. He was in a hurry, so we had only the briefest chat. Anyhow there was little new to discuss—but I did manage to ask him what had happened about Tim Burrows. He gave me a sardonic glance, and said that as they hadn't been in a position to charge him, they'd naturally had to let him go. However, he didn't say that the investigation had ended.

The inquest on Ryland's murder had opened some

days before, but only formal evidence had been taken. In the absence of any close relative, the body had been identified by the commodore of the Springford yacht club; and after the medical evidence had been heard, the police had asked for an adjournment. The resumed hearing—reported at considerable length in the press—occurred a week later, and the known facts of the murder were gone over in detail by police witnesses. I had been a little uneasy in case I might be called to give evidence, but I wasn't, and neither was Tim Burrows, and no mention was made of any confessions. Either there had been a bit of private arranging behind the scenes, or the police themselves had decided to keep mum. Maude told the court that his inquiries were continuing, but that so far there was no reliable evidence as to who the murderer might be. He didn't ask for another adjournment, and the murder verdict was against person or persons unknown.

I couldn't feel absolutely sure that there wouldn't be another knock on my door one day—perhaps quite soon. Higher authority might take a different view from Maude about my involvement. . . . Or, alternatively, that I wouldn't read one day that Tim Burrows had been arrested and charged. . . . But neither of these things happened. The public prosecutor had evidently put the two unsupported confessions in his scales, and decided they were too evenly balanced for action to be taken on either. When you come to think of it, what else could he do?

I was curious to know how Tim had been getting on since his release, and one day I drove down to Springford to find out. Not, I may say, with the intention of seeing him. I would have liked to, but I felt that in all the circumstances it would have been an embarrassing meeting. What I did do was drop in at the local pub, the Anchor, and chat with the landlord and other people in the bar—having first reconnoitered the place to make sure Tim wasn't around. I needn't have worried, because it turned out he was at West Mersea that day, surveying a boat for a client. I was told that he was working hard, that his little yard was flourishing, and that he seemed quite cheerful. It was known in the district, of course, that early on in the Ryland investigation he'd been "helping the police with their inquiries," as the euphemism went; but he had soon been dismissed from the case, and there'd been no further developments. Obviously and wisely, Tim had kept quiet about his "confession"—as I had about mine—and there was no disposition to suspect him of the murder. Even if there had been, I doubt if any of the locals would have blamed him. Being solid and sensible countryfolk, they too believed in justice rather than the law. They had been wholly with Tim over the Kathie affair—and I gathered that quite a lot of them had read the article about Ryland in the *Star* after the murder. The general view in the public bar was that Max Ryland had been an out-and-out stinker who had asked for what he'd got, and that his loss had been the world's gain. Perhaps the same thought had crossed the mind of the public prosecutor!

Kathie, it seemed, had not reappeared in the neighborhood, and it looked as though she was out of Tim's life for good. I was sorry to hear that, but I wasn't particularly surprised. After all the shock and violence, it would have been too much to expect a happy ending to their brief romance. A fresh start, I reflected, was probably the best bet for both of them.

I finished my second pint, had a quick snack at the bar, and then, as the day was sunny and mild for November and Tim was away, I strolled along the seawall to his yard. The houseboat, I saw, had been given a coat of paint—which must have been its first in years. The rills around it were chock-a-block with small craft laid up for the winter, and the saltings were dotted with various bits of work in progress. The place certainly had a much more prosperous appearance than when I'd seen it last. Even the skeptical Maude, I thought, would have had to agree that with all these signs of carefree activity around, the yard didn't look in the least like the habitat of a man with a murder on his mind.

I dropped down on to the saltings and continued along them under the wall for a few hundred yards, enjoying the pale sunshine. The tide was out, and the rills near the wall were narrow, so that walking was no problem. From time to time I stopped to inspect some interesting bit of debris that had been washed up against the wall. There was a dead baby seal—I'd never seen one of those on a beach before—and the remains of a life buoy with an indecipherable ship's name on it, and some odd-shaped shells, and bits of tarred timber, and several empty containers—all the varied flotsam of a high-water mark.

I was about to turn back when my eye was caught by what looked like a piece of cloth, a piece of grayish cloth, protruding from sand and stones. There was a button attached to it, and close to the button there was a brown stain. Suddenly, in my mind, an alarm bell sounded.

What was it that Tim had said in his confession to the police? Something about a bloodstain on the sleeve of a gray shirt. Which he'd tried to remove, without success. So he'd taken the shirt out to the channel, and tied it to a large stone, and sunk it. . . . Could it have come adrift, and been washed up like the other flotsam? Could this be the shirt . . . ? Visible now to any sharp-eyed policeman, pursuing his inquiries around the Burrows yard. . . .

I bent, and pulled on the sleeve, and drew the sodden, discolored object out of its stony bed. It was a shirt, all right—but when I spread it out, I saw with relief that it was a small one, a child's shirt. There was a faded Mickey Mouse picture on the front of it. And the mark on the sleeve was a smear of oil.

I should have known better, I told myself. Tim Burrows wasn't the sort of man to botch a simple job like weighting and sinking a shirt. He was too good with knots. . . .

A week or so after my visit to Springford, I asked Muriel to dine with me again, and we met at a quiet little restaurant in Frith Street. By now I had fully recovered from the strain of all the happenings since Ryland's murder, and was in pretty good spirits. Muriel wanted to know how I had been occupying myself since our last meeting, and why I hadn't been in touch with her. She said she'd telephoned me a couple of times, but I'd been out. I would dearly have liked to tell her the whole story—she'd have made a splendid audience—but of course I didn't. Some secrets have to be firmly locked away, and mine was one of them. I said vaguely that I'd been doing some fieldwork for a new book, and she didn't press me for details. She asked me what I thought of the inquest and the verdict, and so on, and I said I wasn't really surprised the police hadn't been able to bring the murder home to anyone, in view of the vast number of enemies Max must have had. I repeated what I'd said to Maude—that it could easily have been some fellow yachtsman at the marina, someone we knew nothing at all about; or perhaps someone from the film world. . . . Muriel said she'd expected rather more of Maude, considering his obvious ability. She'd quite expected him to solve the case. I said that for all we knew, he *had* solved it, but couldn't prove it—which often happened in these investigations. We left the matter there, and talked of pleasanter things. I spoke enthusiastically of Portugal and recommended Muriel to go there—not, I added, that she looked as though she needed a holiday, she'd never looked better in her life, but I thought she'd find it agreeable. She asked me if I had any plans for going away again, and I said, well, there was just a chance I might have to, but—with fingers firmly crossed under the table—that I didn't think it very likely. I asked her for news of Laura, who was reported in reasonably flourishing condition and enjoying her new job. I didn't attempt to probe—I merely said I was glad she was well. Altogether it was a pleasant, chatty, uninhibited meeting. Muriel was always good company, as I told her, a real tonic, with or without a prescription. We had a lot of laughs, as well as a jolly good dinner.

As I was about to hand her into a taxi afterwards, she suddenly said, "Walter, you've changed."

"Oh?" I said. "How?"

She gave me one of her appraising looks. "I don't quite know. . . . You seem more relaxed, more assured. What's that phrase the Americans use? 'Walking tall' . . . Have you found yourself another girl?"

"You know there's only one girl in my life," I said. "Apart from you, of course."

"Well, there must be something. . . . Have you been working on a particularly good plot?"

I smiled. "I suppose you could say that."

"H'm. You're holding out on me, aren't you? I'm sure something's happened. . . ."

I kissed her cheek, and helped her to squeeze into the cab. "I'm not saying a word, Muriel. Not a word. Except—thanks for everything."

A couple of nights later she telephoned me.

She said, "Walter, I've been talking to Laura. I don't know *quite* what your feelings are now, and I may be putting my big feet right in it—but if you are free of entanglements, and if you are sure you won't try to rush fences, and if you promise not to say stupid things, and of course if you want it to happen—I think she would meet you."

I laughed. "It's a pretty 'iffy' offer, isn't it? But I accept—with all my heart."

"You're sure?" ·

"Quite sure. I can't imagine that either of us has anything to lose by meeting. It's just possible we might have something to gain. But I promise not to bank on it."

"Bless you," Muriel said. "Be nice to her, Walter. Not too nice—but nice. She's been through Hell."

I thought to myself, "Who hasn't?"—but I didn't say it.

Laura came to the house on a Saturday morning, just before noon.

{ 179 }

I had wondered whether it was a good place to meet—whether, since I'd been occupying it alone for more than three months, it was a sufficiently neutral place for the exchanges we were bound to have. Also, whether its associations wouldn't be too upsetting for Laura. I'd suggested to Muriel that perhaps we could use her flat while she was at surgery. But it seemed that Laura preferred to come to the house, and of course I went along with her wishes.

I met her in the drive. She was wearing a smart suit—a suit that greatly became her, and which I hadn't seen before. She was exquisitely groomed and made up—carrying her war paint like an emblazoned shield. She was a little thinner than I remembered her, and there were some tight lines around her mouth that I hadn't observed before. But otherwise she looked just the same—the devastatingly attractive girl I'd fallen head over ears in love with, and in my inadequate fashion had remained in love with. . . .

We approached each other with tentative smiles. Few things can be more difficult than the renewal of contact, after months of separation, with someone you have loved, and parted from in bitterness. There was no question of a kiss, an embrace, a warm affectionate greeting—on either side. And shaking hands would have been ridiculous. So I just said "Hello," and Laura said "Hello" in return. Both of us were self-conscious and constrained.

I said, "Well, come on in," and followed her into the sitting room. I scarcely needed to ask her what she'd like to drink, because I knew. Before lunch, Dubonnet with a little ice. I got the drinks, and we sat down opposite each other and said "Cheers."

Laura looked around. I'd tried to tidy the place up a

bit, but it was still in rather a mess. In her absence I'd treated the whole house as an extension of my study—and the cleaning had been neglected. She pretended not to notice. "You seem to have managed quite well," she said. I shook my head. "I've survived—that's all."

We made some small talk. I asked her where she'd been working. She said that most of the time she'd been at the BBC's Birmingham studio. I asked her whether it was a similar job to the one she'd been doing in London before our marriage, and she said yes, only the people she met were less stimulating. She asked me if I was writing, and I said no, I was just planning. There was an awkward pause. She said, "I think you've put on a little weight, Walter"—which seemed unlikely to me after all my exertions. I said that if I had it must be because I'd consumed so many calories with Muriel. . . .

It couldn't last, of course. One moment we were looking at each other across a huge gulf, estranged and apart. The next, Laura was in tears. "It's all been so humiliating," she said.

I longed to comfort her, to take her in my arms and hold her close to me—but the moment hadn't come, and I didn't know whether it ever would.

"It's been humiliating for me, too," I said. "No one could have been more humiliated than I was by Max—in this house, in this room."

She dabbed at her eyes. "Two humiliations don't seem to offer much of a basis for the repair of a marriage—would you say?"

"I don't know. Perhaps they do. At least we're both in the same boat."

"I'd like to believe it was possible. . . . I feel so—so *lost*."

"I'm ready to search for you," I said.

She smiled through her tears.

"Look," I said, "I've got a suggestion. . . . Let's pretend, for the time being, that nothing whatever has happened in the past few months. Let's put it all on ice. And maybe leave it there. Let's start again from where we left off. We could go somewhere. . . . Tunis would be pleasant in November."

"Do you—do you think it would help?"

"I don't know—but it might. . . . We could make plans over lunch. We could go to that restaurant in Finchley we both liked. How about it?"

"Yes—all right," she said.

I waited for her in the drive while she repaired her face. She had come in her car, the familiar old Rover, so there was no need to get out the station wagon. As she joined me, I started to walk around to the driving seat. Then I stopped.

"I wish you'd drive," I said. "I'm feeling a bit jittery."

She looked at me in surprise. "M'm—Muriel was right. You *have* changed."

On the way to the restaurant, an odd notion struck me. Suppose a thousand people, a cross-section of people who had learned all about us, all about what had happened to us, had been asked in a kind of Gallup poll how they rated our chances of sorting things out, of mending our marriage, of coming together again in happiness— what would they have said?

I thought there would have been an awful lot of "Don't Knows."